CHERISHING WHISKEY'S SALVATION

CHERISHING WHISKEY'S SALVATION

Chrissy Hartmann
Prickle Forrest Books

COPYRIGHT

This is a work of fiction. Names, characters, places, and incidents either are the product of the author's imagination or are used fictitiously. Any resemblance to actual persons, living or dead, events, or locales is entirely coincidental.

Copyright © 2023 by Chrissy Hartmann

All rights reserved. No part of this book may be reproduced or used in any manner without written permission of the copyright owner except for the use of quotations in a book review. For more information, address: chrissyhartmann@sssnet.com

First edition January 2023

Book Cover design by Angelica Hagman
Editing by Rachel Shipp Editing

ISBN 978-1-7379288-3-6 (Paperback)
ISBN 978-1-7379288-2-9 (E-Book/Digital)
ISBN 978-1-7379288-5-0   (Large Print)

www.chrissyhartmann.com

DEDICATION

To my favorite guys — K.O., Jacob, Dad, Ed, and Brady
"Love and thanks for all your help!"

ACKNOWLEDGEMENTS

I would love to send you all a dozen red roses and a bottle of champagne. Instead, though, you will have to be satisfied with my undying love and grateful thanks for your support whether it be by encouragement, praise, plot developing, editing, and even the tedious process of helping design the book cover. Never let it be said that I didn't appreciate the help.

Big heartfelt thanks and love to:
My hubby and son whose undying belief in my writing once again pushed me to the publish button.

Mom and Dad's support regarding my artistic talent, my brothers opinions and suggestions regarding the hero of this novella, and my sisters who if it hadn't been for their help with editing, I would have nothing but blank pages.

My writing besties of the Wayne Novelist Guild, who inspire me every time we talk.

My editors and beta readers — Cary, Cyndi, Ruth, Tracy, and Rachel — thanks for your positive words and knowledge of the craft. I heard it all, and it meant something.

I want to especially thank my good friend, Mark Beckler, who shared his knowledge regarding all things dealing with helicopters and aviation in general. If you had not shared your expertise, this hop would not have been possible.

But most of all, I want to thank God because without him I would not be able to do any of this.

Love to you all!

Chapter 1 Whiskey Duty

IF YOU KNEW CHARLIE STOCKTON, you might wonder who or what held his heart. Even Charlie would admit he didn't know. And today, wouldn't be any different from any other. Well, sort of.

As Charlie stood on a raised wooden boardwalk on the outskirts of Austin with his scuffed boots brushing against a polished rail, in the not too far distant blue sky of puffy white clouds, a chopping whirl of wind came from three helicopters—two on the flanks and one following behind.

He removed his brown Stetson and wiped his brow on the sleeve of his coat all while staring at the scene moving toward him. At first, when one looked they might think it in slow motion, but not possible when Charlie took in all the folks scurrying around him for a closer look for themselves.

A slight quirk of the cowboy's lips on one side curled upward.

A low thunder rattled the planks he stood on.

A couple brushed past him with two small children to get up close to the banister.

He watched the children peer through the rail and squeal in delight.

"Look. They're coming."

He stuffed his hat back on his head and rocked back in his boots as his calloused hands pushed his jacket away from his waist to rest. He nodded in silent agreement with the child.

Up ahead on the street, not only were there three black choppers coming, but they followed a herd of Texas longhorns ambling their way with a handful of cowboys on horseback steering them down the street to their destination.

Reminds me of the old days.

Another older cowboy sidled up next to him. "Howdy, Charlie." He checked his watch. "Looks like they're coming just in time."

Charlie nodded with a smile.

The older cowboy with a full head of gray hair smirked. "You miss it?"

Charlie, who himself only had a touch of gray whispering around the edges of his dark brown hair stood taller than the man next to him in what some might describe as a military stance. Yes, a Military stance, but one at ease. He turned his head. The hand that he had clenched against his leg relaxed as he tipped his hat back with one finger. Charlie gave a shrug with one shoulder then turned back to the street. "Not sure what you mean."

The older cowboy laughed as he slapped Charlie's shoulder. "Don't worry, I won't tell Susan."

With the other cowboy's words, a bit of a rascally grin tugged at Charlie's lips.

Charlie loved serving in the military. After all, he did it for thirty plus years. But he loved his ranch that lay just outside of San Antonio too. When he took leave, he always came home to check on the Stockyard. The brains it took to run the ranch and rank in the Army as a Colonel had to take smarts. And with the success Charlie had in both, he definitely had the brains. However, he did have the perfect partner who helped—his wife. And yes, his wife, Susan managed most of the day-to-day finances, but she never made a major decision without Charlie's opinion. Yes, it did help too that she, herself had the brains for business too. After all, she carried the title of CEO of the Mae Foundation, a top one-hundred company, a leading cosmetic company to boot. The business world knew she took the Mae Foundation over when her own mamma died and made it into a huge success. In fact, it ranked as one of the world's leading cosmetic companies, which very few of these types of businesses ever came as close to her success in the industry. So successful, it ranked on the top Fortune one-hundred list. And the Stockyard? Well, within the past ten years, it had become one of the most profitable beef sellers in the states. And Charlie thanked his lucky stars he had such an intelligent woman for a business partner. Better yet, his wife.

Charlie turned his head only slightly to get a better view from the corner of his eye. The grin of pride he wore grew just a little more noticeable. "Good to know, Hank."

"I guess it's hard for some folks to return to everyday life, but we sure are glad you're back on a permanent basis."

Charlie laughed. "You sure about that? Or are you just glad you don't have to deal with Susan anymore?"

Hank grabbed Charlie's upper arm and jostled it. "Okay, Colonel, you got me there. Not that we had trouble with Susan—"

"But?"

Hank rubbed at his jaw. "But, I'll admit, it's good to have you back full time."

Charlie nodded. A bit of warmth pulled at his heart along with some humor.

Warmth for the friendship he had maintained with these ranchers for the past forty some years, but if he had to admit it, the humor he found in their appreciation of his return to ranching had to be because they found Susan more stubborn than he. In business, she rarely ever gave in, hence the success with the Stockyard and Mae Foundation.

Charlie chuckled to himself knowing that these good old cowboys thought they were going to run roughshod over his wife. And to their misfortune, they never came anywhere close to it.

"Nice to know somebody appreciates my hard work."

He then returned his gaze to the sky.

The helicopters rotated position. The chopper on the left broke rank to help one cowboy on horseback chase a stray back into the herd while the trailing chopper repositioned itself on the now empty flank.

Charlie flexed his fingers. His head dipped in approval. That maneuver reminded him of the last few months of patrolling the Texas border looking for coyotes and their unexpected prey. He let out his breath as the steer joined the herd once more.

Hank turned, but first threw out one of his elbows to Charlie's side. "The vote is at three o'clock sharp. Don't be late."

Charlie patted his friend's shoulder. "Yes, Sir."

The longhorns meandered their way past him. The couple at the rail with the young kids turned to leave. Charlie noticed the dad wore a short cut close to his scalp. Not necessarily standard issue, but close. Probably a soldier on leave, after all, Texas had a number of military bases in the state and quite a few Military families settled nearby.

Charlie nodded to the mom then the dad.

The young couple smiled with the dad's smile wide. "Colonel, good seeing you out."

Charlie again nodded with the slight lift of one eyebrow. Not exactly sure, who he nodded at, but it became obvious to him that the man recognized him. Charlie tried to place him, but nothing registered. Nevertheless, Charlie believed all soldiers needed recognized and he had never been too high up the ladder to make sure they all got due recognition. "Thank you. Now, if you'll excuse me, I've got business to take care of."

The young dad nodded with a two-finger salute.

Charlie pivoted in his boots. Boots he preferred more than the military issue he wore for the past thirty years unless he took leave. But now retired he wore them every day, a prerogative he thoroughly enjoyed. After all, the cowboy blood that ran through his veins came from a long line of cowboys or as he liked to refer to himself as a cattle rancher. And no one labeled Charlie as just any old rancher. In fact, most in Texas recognized the name if not the fact that he owned one of the largest ranches near San Antonio and the east coast. Anyone who looked at his birth certificate would find the name Charles Joseph Stockton, but his friends called him Charlie. Some went as far as calling him Colonel Charlie, but not for the way he could get things done with his iron fist for ranching.

No, it stuck because Charlie had been in the United States Army, specifically the 104th surveillance and 13th attack squadron. A squadron who flew helicopters from San Antonio to the Gulf Coast even did a stint or two to such faraway places to help Special Forces out in Mogadishu.

But doing that stint almost cost him his life, so when he recovered, he found himself stationed back near San Antonio as a UH-72 Lakota chopper pilot who cruised up and down the Texas border searching for coyotes and mule crossers who traveled into Texas without Uncle Sam's approval — not a force to reckon with. And after a few missions of patrolling the border, Charlie had come to the decision shortly before his fiftieth birthday that it had come time to change careers. After all, he did own one of the largest cattle ranches in Texas, and not to mention a beautiful bride and daughter he missed spending part of the last thirty years with. And frankly, after his near death-experience into Mogadishu, the air-filled skies with bullets and smoke no longer appealed to him.

Anyway, he needed to get back home and take care of business. Plus the fact that he had been skipped over for the rank of general stuck in his craw. So, if the military did not want him as one of their top military men, then he would go where they needed him, back home to his cattle ranch — The Stockyard, just outside San Antonio. A ranch with a huge spread that needed someone to manage it with a strong hand and respect. Not that his wife did a bad job, but the running of two successful businesses took a lot of hard work and with the ranch gaining more success and the demand high for his beef, it seemed more practical to retire and get back to ranching. But most of all, he could not let his wife do it all. It would eventually take its toll on her and Charlie had his responsibilities to her and their daughter. He had put those on hold for thirty years for the most part and now the time had come to get back to them. Plus since the Military did not want him any further up in rank, then, he figured they needed him less than the two most important people in his life did.

Therefore, when someone referred to him as the Colonel, they were not exactly wrong, but in all honesty, Colonel Charles Joseph Stockton preferred the moniker of rancher, Charlie Stockton, best. Oh sure, if he knocked back a few beers or better yet Barleyshot Whiskey, the Colonel side came out a bit more, but Charlie rarely let that side come out. Unless of course, he managed to hook up with his best buddy, Jack Barleyshot — AKA Colonel Barleyshot came to town. Then watch out.

The two could stir up trouble just about anywhere. All innocent trouble, but trouble no matter what. And anyway, Mogadishu had been years ago and those were times he no longer thought about.

Nope, Charlie only liked to think about the daily happenings with the ranch and his family. And at the age of fifty plus, he preferred the long rolling pastures with steers on it rather than gun smoked skies and flying bullets.

Charlie smiled with his head dipping in slight agreement with the choppers formation. Not too close, but not far enough away they could not get a reading on the scene below.

The man brought his gaze back to the street. Over the tops of his sunglasses, not prescription sunglasses either, As he had perfect vision unless of course he stared into the Texas sun, which at the moment he could not help as it sat high in the sky at the noontime hour. He tipped back his Stetson with one rough finger. And From what anyone could see from his viewpoint, if they looked down the makeshift street just outside the newly built convention center near Austin, they might think they were in an old Western town watching John Wayne herding a group of cattle through the street But not Charlie Stockton, because he knew what the East Coast Cattle Ranchers Association planned for this year's cattle trade show.

This year they brought cattle to the show. Yes most understood they always brought cattle, but not longhorns, But then again this year's cattle trade show had promised to be different. Their plan seemed to work for the most part with the Attendance tripling this year.

Charlie smiled at the good fortune.

He might have suggested the idea, but there were plenty other ranchers who would have come up with an idea if not a better one. And on the whole, it brought everyone out. After all, who would not like to see a real-life herd of cattle amble down the main street? And if the longhorn cattle did not draw some interest, then maybe the new technology of using the helicopters would.

The lopsided curl of Charlie's lips rose another notch.

He flew similar ones like these before — Lakota's, and the whirling sound of any chopper always energized him. His hands opened and closed as if they ached to maneuver the controls. He shook his head and reminded himself.

Those days are long gone. Now, it's all about the cattle.

But the mechanical birds always made his heart kick.

The helicopters followed the cattle from the rear to both sides making sure the cattle would not stray. They were another rancher's private little air force that were used to maintain the vast property along the border who just so happened to owe Charlie a favor and once in a while they patrolled for unwanted trespassers like coyotes, etc.

Charlie glanced down at the cattle trade show's itinerary. The schedule on it said they would be voting at three o'clock for those who were heading up the committee on the cost of beef. A committee formed out of necessity to help stave off the inflated prices of beef because the cattle ranchers did not want to suffer another blow to the industry like they had suffered years back with a certain Midwest daytime talk show host who attacked their cattle prices. So since Charlie had a lot of success with his ranch now that he had return a year or so ago, the other ranchers decided with the success he had in building his ranch into a more profitable one, they wanted him to head up this committee. And today, they would vote on it. Not one to avoid problems, he usually stepped up to help, if not lead the charge. Sure, it would not excite him as pulling out downed troops out of Mogadishu, but it would challenge him nonetheless. And Charlie Stockton never backed away from that sort of thing.

The herd of cattle kicked up clouds of dirt as they passed the crowd.

Charlie held onto his breath for a moment. The dust only made him thirsty along with the rising heat. He would enjoy a coffee right now to parch his thirst, but in this crowd, the chances of him finding a vendor selling some were slim to none. He scanned the skyline down toward the conference center. Just above the building stood a lit sign announcing the new hotel that would host most those who traveled to the conference — the Hilux. He licked his lips in anticipation of a good hot fresh cup of coffee once he checked in.

One of the cowboys rode by. A few of the onlookers distracted him from his thoughts of coffee when they cheered for the mystical-looking boys on horseback who kept the four-legged long-horned troublemakers from breaching the crowd.

Charlie did some of his own cheering. Well, cheering to himself that the entertainment seemed to go on without a hitch. IN all reality, he conjured up the idea half-heartedly from a time when he and his best buddy sat on a balcony in Pamplona and watched the daring Spaniards try to outrun the bulls. But not one for promoting a goring type of celebration, he thought a somewhat old-fashioned cattle roundup would help draw more people into the trade show. He smiled and pushed up on his sunglasses. Ready to pivot on his boot heel, he froze with the light touch on his forearm. Not wanting to stay and chat, as he needed to find where the voting would take place, plus, a cup of coffee.

He told himself to make it quick. Probably only someone who needed directions.

When he turned back from the area he stood, he cocked his head. One of his silver chestnut streaked eyebrow's rose. With the sun, hitting the newcomer from behind, Charlie realized the person would not ask for directions. In fact, he had known the man for quite some years as they both owned cattle ranches and sat on some of the same committees. "Howdy Bill. I figured I'd run into you sooner or later."

The man dressed in fancy boots and suit with a beard, which rivaled old St. Nick's, rubbed at his whiskers. "Howdy Charlie. Haven't seen you since the Cattleman's Ball last December."

Charlie flashed his white teeth at that memory. His heart gave a little kick when the image of Susan in her black evening gown and heels pressed up against him.

As if he were relaying a secret, Bill leaned closer. "In fact, never expected to see you here today."

Charlie dropped both arms to his side with one hand curled around the itinerary. He rocked back on his boot heels. "Is that so?"

The man nodded. "Sure didn't. Not especially after hearing about the fire."

Charlie's gut dropped. His eyes widen and his brows stretch up past the rim of his sunglasses. His boots rocked forward onto the balls of his feet. His empty hand shot out and grasped the other man's arm.

"Fire? What fire?"

"Liz called me earlier to tell me she saw a post on the San Antonio Insider Facebook page that the fire department sent one of those pumper trucks, a ladder truck, and even an ambulance to your ranch."

"My ranch? Are you sure?"

Bill cocked a bushy white eyebrow. "Unless, you soled the Stockyard in the past few days, yes, your ranch."

Spiked tingles ran from Charlie's neck to his heart. Not ones that might make him throw up, but ones that seemed to have wrapped themselves around his heart and dug in deep. He nodded to his friend. "How long ago were they spotted there?"

Bill rubbed his jaw. The movement of his scratch that jostled the white curls would normally make one lose their concentration, but not for Charlie, at least not for what crashed around in his head. With his experience as a Colonel and a helicopter pilot, he had experienced many trying situations and losing his cool on the outside would not make anything better. So drawing on his strength as a soldier, he decided it would be best to get more details before he made any rash decisions. But it did not mean he could stop his thoughts from going into overdrive. And at the moment, that's exactly where they headed.

Susan? Did she go into the office today? And what about Evie? Where's Evie? Why haven't I heard from anyone? Need to get a hold of Susan.

Charlie raised his eyes to heaven.

Oh, Lord. Please tell me they are okay. I'll lose the ranch over them. Just don't let me lose them. Amen.

The other cowboy frowned as he patted Charlie's forearm. "Now, don't you worry. I told Liz not to believe everything she saw on those social media sites. For lands sake man, you don't know if what they put on there might be true or not. In fact, they're no better than those gossip rags one finds at the supermarket."

"She saw this on one of those social media pages then? Is that what you're saying?"

Bill nodded. "Yes. If it were real bad, don't you think they would put it on the news?"

Charlie thought about it for a minute. Bill did have a good point. And after all, why would not Susan have called him.

So maybe it's not as bad as Bill's wife is making it out to be?

But just in case, Charlie made a mental note to find out as soon as he could head for the hotel.

Bill dragged his hand down through his whiskers. "Liz says one report suspected a false alarm." Bill cocked an eyebrow. " And come to think of it, she also texted that the post didn't have any real pictures of the San Antonio Fire Department at the scene. So if there had been a fire, doubt it caused much damage."

At those words, the barbed-like tightness around Charlie's heart lessened slightly.

"No trucks at the barns then?"

The man smiled. "No, heavens no. Liz said there were no pictures of the barns."

If not the barns, then the house? Now that set a whole new set of worries upon him.

Charlie groaned. Then as if he could see through the miles that separated he and the ranch, questions of what kind of damage and who or what exactly had caused this flooded his thoughts.

He snapped out of his contemplation when the older gentleman squeezed his shoulder. "Now don't you worry, Charlie. Everything's going to be fine. But you better get a hold of Susan, especially if she doesn't follow those social media pages." Bill pulled on a few of the curly strands of his beard. "And Evie? Hopefully Susan's got her so busy she's not taken up cooking again." The old man let out a deep barrel chuckle. "But, if you think about it, why would she want to cook when you have Lucia?"

Charlie contemplated those words.

And yeah, why would Evie be cooking if Lucia held the position of their housekeeper who did all the cooking? She hadn't gone on vacation, had she?

In fact, Charlie could not remember the last time she scheduled a vacation, yet alone, received a raise from him. And the woman had talent, which meant none of them ever went hungry. He made a note to check the payroll to see the last time she received a raise. Maybe he'd better reward her for her outstanding employment. After all, dedicated and deserving people should reap rewards for their hard work.

As if to prevent Charlie from rehashing his thoughts that obviously leaned toward his own work history for the past thirty years, a chopper flew past him with a swirling wind in their wake. His hat lifted. But not distracted enough and with plenty of experience around helicopters and what they did to hats, he managed a two-finger grasp of his Stetson before it blew down the street.

Charlie chuckled at his talent for keeping a hold of his hat, but nothing could replace the stick stuck in his craw with regards to the whole way his retirement came about from the Military. He blew out his breath.

"You got a point there."

"Why, yes I do. Lucia is probably the best cook around."

Bill ruffled his beard. "If you find you need to displace Lucia until you get things repaired, don't hesitate to let her know, she's more than welcome to lend a hand over at my ranch."

But if there actually had been a fire and the housekeeper's cooking had not caused the fire, then who or how did it start?

Stone faced with a frown trying to push through, Charlie gripped the rolled itinerary almost crushing it between his fingers.

Nice try, but Lucia does more than cook for me. Not happening.

Charlie rolled his eyes. "Yeah, sure. I'll let her know."

Bill slapped Charlie on the back with a grin. "You best get a hold of Susan and check on Evie." Then he pointed down the street toward the convention center. "I'll see you in there to vote. Remember three o'clock sharp."

On those words, Charlie nodded as his stomach sank.

"Oh lord, please tell me Evie had nothing to do with this."

Charlie: Darlin', you okay?

Charlie: Susan, answer me!

Susan: You do realize I'm quite busy right now, don't you?

Charlie: What the blazes happened?

Susan: Enjoying your conference? Chaos here.

Charlie: Sorry, Darlin, but tell me what you've heard.

Susan: Firetrucks are at the ranch.

Charlie: And?

Susan: And there was a fire.

Charlie: Susan!

Susan: Charles!

Charlie: What caught fire?

Susan: The kitchen. I'll be heading there shortly.

Charlie: Everyone okay?

Susan: For the moment yes.

Charlie: The moment? How did this happen?

Susan: You really want to know?

Charlie: Yes. What caused it?

Susan: Are you serious? Do you really not know?

Charlie: Stop playing games and tell me.

Susan: Have you spoken to your daughter?

Charlie: "My" daughter?

Susan: Yes. Aren't you the one who tells her to try new things?

Charlie: Well, I might have said something like that once.

Susan: Once? Really?

Charlie: Okay, maybe twice. But is our daughter okay?

Susan: Argh! Yes. For the time being.

Charlie: What's that mean?

Susan: Who else do you know that can't cook?

Susan: Charles?

Charlie: Hold on, I'm thinking.

Susan: Seriously?

Charlie: By your tone, I'm guessing the blame goes to our daughter.

Susan: Brilliant deduction Sherlock!

Charlie: Now Darlin, hold that temper.

Susan: Temper? Are you serious? You want me to hold my temper? If
            you only knew what I had to do today, you'd not ask me to
            hold my temper.

Charlie: Can you handle this?

Susan: I run a Fortune 100 company, are you really asking me that
            question or are you trying to be a jackass?

Charlie: No. Don't hang our daughter before I get home. Okay?

Susan: Well, bless your heart. Aren't you asking a lot?

Charlie: Remember our vows—for better or worse. Promise me you
            won't do anything drastic.

Charlie: Susan?

Susan: Okay fine. You got till the end of the convention.

Charlie: Wait. What else are you dealing with?

Susan: I'll tell you once you get home.

Charlie: No. Tell me now.

Susan: I'll send pictures tonight.

Charlie: Pictures? You have pictures?

Susan: Yes. The fire department will be sending some to me.

Charlie: Wait. What are you talking about now?

Susan: The fire. What are you talking about?

Charlie: Never mind.

Susan: Never mind about what?

Charlie: The other matter.

Susan: But there's no pictures regarding that matter.

Charlie: I'm getting a headache. Need to find some aspirin.

Susan: Ask the Concierge.

Charlie: For pictures?

Susan: No. Aspirin.

Charlie: But what about these pictures?

Susan: I'll send them once I get them.

Charlie: Susan?

Susan: Don't you want to see the damage?
Charlie: No, Darlin. Don't go to any trouble. Surprise me when I get
            home.
Susan: Grrr.
Charlie: Got to go, voting starts soon. Love you.
Charlie: Susan?
Susan: Yes, fine. Love to you too.

Chapter 2 Whiskey Rot

THE DOOR SWUNG OPEN. A hint of fresh flowers and cool air drifted forward. Charlie walked into his hotel room at the Austin Hilux only to stop and glance around at his accommodations. With him, a bellhop followed in his wake carrying a medium-sized grey suitcase. Charlie glanced around the hotel suite. The king-sized bed lay on one side of the room decorated in dark browns with cream and tan accenting the details. Details like the pile of pillows that covered the top third of the bed. He shook his head.

No person needs that many pillows.

The flash of an image of his wife propped up with one of those come-hither looks by the mountain of pillows bolted across his brain. Charlie smiled.

Well, not unless you got yourself the best damn woman in Texas.

The whoosh of the full-length mirrored closet door sliding open broke him from his thoughts of the bed. He scanned more of the room. An armoire sat at one end encasing the sixty-four inch digital TV. With a small settee and two wingback chairs in shades of brown and cream huddled up close to the glass coffee table as if they held court. A bouquet of mixed flowers sat atop it perfuming the air with a fragrance of vanilla, lavender, orange blossom, and lilacs.

"Mr. Stockton, I'll just set your suitcase in the closet for you."

Charlie tossed the small carryon duffle bag on to the coffee table. Then, he reached into his pocket. He pulled out a roll of cash and peeled off two of the bills. He stepped toward the other man.

The bellhop pointed back toward the small group of furniture. "The remote for the TV is on the coffee table and the minibar is stocked."

Not ready to hand over a tip for helping, Charlie scanned the room again. Unable to find the item he wanted, he turned back to the young man. "What about coffee?"

The bellhop smiled. "Just call room service and they can bring it up to you."

Charlie removed his Stetson and tossed it next to another similar but smaller arrangement of flowers onto a three-drawer dresser just outside the closet. "I hope they're quick about it."

The bellhop danced back and forth with a nervous nod of his head. "I keep telling them we need to put those single-serve coffee makers in each room."

Charlie nodded. "That would probably be a good idea."

"Yeah, that's what I thought, but I'm just the bellhop. They don't listen to me."

"Well, they should. It's a good idea."

The bellhop grinned. "Thank you Sir. If you need anything else, don't hesitate to call the front desk. I'm on duty all night."

The young man moved toward the open door. When he reached the threshold, he stepped out and turned for the elevator.

Charlie grabbed the edge of the door before it closed. "Hold up a second. Here's for your help."

The bellhop halted with a sheepish grin. "Thank you, Sir. I appreciate your kindness."

Charlie flashed a smile. "Likewise."

"Enjoy your stay, Mr. Stockton."

Charlie eased the door closed. "I plan on doing that." Then pivoting on one boot, he headed straight for the bedside table. The room's phone sat next to a small directory and what looked like a complimentary note pad and pen with the hotel's moniker on it.

Not needing the pen or notepad, Charlie grabbed the directory, which only turned out to be a sheet of paper with names and numbers listed on one side of the tri-fold sections. An advertisement for a steak house, the Red Star Steakhouse to be exact.

"Not a steak house I'll be sampling this time."

He shook his head. Because for this convention, he would not have time to check out the other steak houses around. He knew he should, but with the fire, he could not waste time. Susan expected him home as soon as possible to help with the mess. So for this convention, he had to cut it short, get the business done, and eat here at the hotel. After all, the hotel helped sponsor this year's convention and the menu would feature their beef.

Since his curiosity still had his attention, he flipped the last fold over and found what he expected — an advertisement for Barleyshot Whiskey.

He smiled. "Well done Jack but next time, get it on the first fold. Not the last one."

Almost positive Evie would tell him the same thing, he thought about having her give Jack's advertising department a few lessons about how, when, and where to set their campaign. But then as if he wanted to smack himself upside the head, he reminded himself that Evie worked for Susan. And if his bride caught him farming Evie's expertise on the matter out to someone else, she'd probably have him lynched from the nearest hayloft.

Now he chuckled out loud — a dry, rough laugh, which made his face pucker with the sound.

Got to get something to drink.

Once more, he studied the room. No signs of any coffee machine. Only the minibar looked to be the source of any kind of immediate refreshment, but he had no hankering for anything else other than coffee.

A low growl rolled from Charlie's throat activating the quick dexterity of his fingers. He maneuvered the tri-folded piece of paper back to its original shape. Dial zero for the front desk, one for security, two for housekeeping, and three for the bar and restaurant. He tossed the pamphlet down and picked up the receiver. The cord unraveled stretching to allow him to put it up to his ear without bending over. Charlie pressed the number three button and waited for someone to answer.

A monotone buzz rang once, then twice, and on the third ring, a voice sounded. Charlie rolled his neck. The muscles grew tight. He licked his lips. "Howdy. This is Charlie Stockton in room 311. I'd like to order a pot of coffee."

He waited a second then tapping a finger on the desk, he shook his head. "No, just black. Nothing fancy."

His free hand rubbed at his jaw. "Twenty minutes?" He paused. "Yes, but put a rush on it if you can." For a split second, Charlie thought about asking for some aspirin, but figured he would not have much luck at getting a bottle or getting it and the coffee before the meeting at three. "Okay, twenty minutes, sure."

He glanced over at the other bedside table. A digital clock glowed. He frowned. Lunch passed well over an hour ago and dinner only hovered on the horizon. So why the hold up on coffee? But not one to complain, he'd just place the order and pray it came sooner.

"Yes, thank you. Room 311."

After giving his thanks, Charlie turned back to the nightstand and cradled the phone receiver on the base. Not sure what to do now, he pivoted and scanned the room.

One of his eyebrows rose as he studied the bed. He contemplated lying down, but with not much time until the vote, he dared not to put his head down on one of the overstuffed pillows. Plus with the image of Susan lying back on the bed with all those pillows, hovered at the back of his thoughts, which in turn made him wonder if there were details Susan bothered not to burden him with since he had no way of helping at the moment. Or maybe she really did not know the whole story yet either. And Charlie needed the details. So he'd just have to wait for them, which by all rights would make him just want to go back home. So for the moment, he needed to concentrate on what he had come to Austin for—the conference and the committee he had been asked to run for regarding the beef prices.

But this would not be easy, especially with guilt pushing at his thoughts making his slight headache raise to a whole new level. He rubbed at his temples with the hopes that he could rub the worry out of his head. It did fade somewhat, but probably because after his text message with Susan he had the understanding that she and Evie were okay, maybe not the kitchen though, but that could easily be replaced.

Charlie released his breath while his heart squeezed. The tightness in his chest would only make the guilt worse if he did nothing but rehash the little facts that he knew. So instead, he wandered over to one of the wingback chairs and dropped into it. He glanced back toward the digital clock. The timepiece informed him he had at least an hour before he needed to head out. He tapped his fingers against the armrest. Then as if he hit some imaginary switch, the sting of prickles formed at the base of his neck.

The prickles moved up. Charlie looked in the direction of the bathroom. He shook his head hoping he could shake off the prickles, but they held on. He cursed under his breath for not stopping at the hotel's gift shop for some aspirin before he checked in.

With his allotted time running out before he had to go and vote, instead of rambling around the hotel to find aspirin, he spotted the TV remote and picked it up.

Maybe a distraction would help.

He pressed the power button. The screen came to life with what he figured to be a local channel for Austin.

The tingles lingered.

He sat back with remote in one hand while he tried to roll the tingles away. No such luck. He watched the screen for a minute. Commercials for trucks, windows, and a few restaurants popped up on the screen. Nothing really to hold his attention. He turned the volume down and dropped the remote onto his lap. The glance toward the clock resulted in more frustration. He still had plenty of time before the coffee would arrive. He sat back and dug his fingers into his neck. A flash of scenery on the TV caught his eye. He picked up the remote and turned up the volume. A channel six banner stared boldly at him — a news update signaled for viewing attention. With his attention perked, Charlie's back stiffened. A weather forecaster appeared in front of a digital map of Texas. The forecaster announced the temperatures would vary with wild swings as a new storm front headed in toward the state from the Gulf of Mexico.

Charlie rubbed his jaw.

Not a blue northerner, but that's not looking good either.

Then with the blink of an eye, another person stood next to the forecaster. This person stood just about chin high and had a perky bounce to their presentation.

Charlie cocked his head. Obviously, with the person's pep, they were not there to talk about the weather. He aimed the remote ready to press the button to move on to the next channel, but a dated image appeared on the screen, an image that definitely caught his eye. He narrowed in on the picture.

His fingers loosened on the remote. He shook his head. Disbelief swamped his brain. All thoughts of coffee evaporated. He stood without much thought as if he moved on some unspoken command. He navigated around the glass coffee table that blocked his direct path to the TV.

His steps halted an arm's length from the images. Not distracted by the banter of chitchat between the two on the screen, Charlie narrowed his gaze onto the image, but not just any image. This image would be none other than that of a clown. And by the clench of Charlie's jaw, not just a random clown either.

A vein along his chin popped. A low growl of words pried their way out of his mouth.

"What's this SOB getting press time for? Hopefully, he's dead."

The background image changed to a fortyish-looking man in an orange jumpsuit.

The hairs on Charlie's neck stood like pitchforks.

The peppy newscaster threw a thumb over her shoulder. "Tonight at six we'll have more news on this breaking story. But in case you've forgotten, this once-young man had kidnapped Texas' only double heiress, the young Evie Mae Stockton, heiress to the Stockton cattle ranch and a Fortune one-hundred company, Mae Foundation on her eighth birthday."

"Son of a…"

A few more pictures of the man shot across the screen.

"He's not dead."

A new image appeared. Actually, an old familiar image appeared. An image of an agitated clown holding a bouquet of balloons. An image that Charlie would not forget. Not this image of Miguel Santos. The Miguel Santos. The Miguel Santos who kidnapped his daughter at eight years old. Charlie's teeth slammed together only allowing for the low growl to slip between his lips. He yanked his cell phone from his jacket. He stabbed the screen. The phone lit up with all its aps on the front. He searched for the calendar. He shook his head once he realized the date correct. His head snapped back up to the TV.

He stared at the news reporter.

"Tonight, at six, I'll be reporting on this oldie but goody story. One that dates back twenty years."

Charlie white knuckled his phone.

The entertainment reporter continued. "As you might remember, one Miguel Santos kidnapped one of Texas's richest families' daughter twenty years ago in an attempt to ransom the eight-year-old little girl for a cash payment he needed to get out from the debt he owed the Mexican cartel."

She pointed to her watch. "Like clockwork, he's up for parole once more. And rumors have it this might be his year to get out from underneath his fifty plus year sentencing. But rumors also say it could be the doings of some politically motivated do-gooders who think he's paid his debt to society. But we here at channel 6 want to know if the Stockton family agrees. So stay tuned for our update at six."

Charlie growled again. "I'll see him rot first."

Text Message

April 20th
1:20 PM

Charlie: You got time to talk?

Jack: Depends.

Charlie: On what?

Jack: You talking by phone? Or over a steak and bottle of whiskey?

Charlie: Still in Austin. Leaving on the 23rd.

Jack: Can it wait? Trouble here on my end with Jillian.

Charlie: She okay?

Jack: No. Fading fast. Need to find Griff.

Charlie: Holy smokes. How can I help?

Jack: Nothing. Appreciate the offer.

Charlie: You sure?

Jack: Unfortunately, only a brother and son can do this.

Charlie: I'll add her to my prayers. Call me if I can help.

Jack: Everything okay?

Charlie: Nothing my 45 can't solve.

Jack: How about some whiskey instead?

Charlie: That would probably work.

Jack: Okay. First bottle is on me.

Charlie: Plan on two.

Jack: That bad?

Charlie: Committee for the beef prices won't settle on the pricing.

Jack: They're idiots. Pull rank on them.

Charlie: Would love to.

Jack: So, why don't you?

Charlie: Not that easy.

Jack: Chicken!

Charlie: We're talking beef, not chicken.

Jack: Bock. Bock. Bawk!

Charlie: Some foreign investors want our beef.

Jack: Foreign investors?

Charlie: Yeh. All our beef. They're offering a good penny for it.
Jack: We need tariffs.
Charlie: I know. Got a few calls into my connections in D.C.
Jack: Ha! Good luck with that.
Charlie: Thanks. Now need to handle this clown thing.
Jack: Clown? The clown?
Charlie: Yes.
Jack: Aim for the heart.
Charlie: Thanks.
Jack: Anytime.
Charlie: Don't tempt me.
Jack: Sorry, but got my own problems. Otherwise, I'd load your clips.
Charlie: Jack?
Jack: Jillian's fading quick. Griff's fighting it.
Charlie: Remember, the Lord only takes the best.
Jack: Thanks, brother.
Charlie: Probably why we survived Mogadishu
Jack: Change of plans, bringing three bottles.
Charlie: Stay strong.

Chapter 3 Whiskey Switch

A WAFT OF JET FUEL AND OIL SATURATED THE AIR AROUND CHARLIE. He stepped out from the private airfield's office with his brown Stetson in one hand and a small beat-up leather carryon slung over his shoulder.

The Texas sun remained high in the sky. The shimmering rays danced all around the airfield as it maneuvered its way around the shadows cast from the hangers and waiting planes. The squint he made as he stepped further away from the building finally pushed him to reach for his sunglasses. Pulling out the ones from his bag that hung off his shoulder, he slipped them over his nose. Immediately, his neck muscles relaxed. Then with his other hand, he placed his Stetson atop his head.

A low rumble turned his attention toward the airstrip. From almost half a football field's length away, a Gulfstream G650 taxied west down the runway.

The hydraulic whoosh of a large metal door sliding open came from a hanger just off to his left. A crew of booted footsteps dashed to the right. Charlie studied the small squad dressed in maintenance flight suits. They carried a fuel hose and other paraphernalia — their destination, the Bell 206 jet ranger — his private chopper.

One of the maintenance guys reached Charlie's luxury whirlybird before the others and pulled out a medium-sized gray suitcase, pivoted, and headed in the direction Charlie traveled. Like a college running back, he tucked the suitcase under his arm as if he headed for the goal line. Charlie's step did not waiver, maybe slowed as not sure of what the young man would do with his luggage. But with the last minute two-step dance he did at the back of the limo, he could not say whether or not his suitcase might get spiked into the trunk. To his surprise, the crew worker adjusted it as if he were laying a babe into a cradle. And on that note, with his bag tucked into the back of the limo, the trunk door shut, the maintenance crewman shot like a bullet back toward the chopper.

Wow. *Need to figure out how to bottle that.*

Finally, he turned his attention back to the limo — The Mae Foundation limo. A vehicle at the top of its class. If Charlie remembered correctly, Susan picked out something quite similar to the Governor's limo. Nothing like the President's Beast, but oddly enough quite similar with its Cadillac-style design and run-flat Goodyear tires, although without the Kevlar. Sure, it had no armor plates to fend off missals, but it had a driver who knew how to operate the thing if any trouble came their way. Susan never seemed to spare any expense for that. And in all reality, it did not bother Charlie that she wanted the best to travel in.

As he approached the car, the grip he had on his small leather flight bag loosened.

The limo's driver door opened. A muscular driver in black suit and mirrored aviators stood. He adjusted his glasses then walked around the back of the car tapping on the backside to ensure its closure.

On Charlie's approach, the familiar face brought a sense of relief. Not that he found the week's stay regarding the cattle convention difficult, he had come to love the ranch. A military lifestyle kept one on the move constantly and to his own surprise, he no longer cared for it. And he found that he disliked business traveling, unless of course he flew his own personal chopper. That particular aspect of the Military would always stick with him.

About two steps from the limo's back door, he found himself next to the driver. He nodded. "Howdy, Sam."

The driver's lips quirked to one side. "Colonel."

"All quiet on the western front?"

Sam said nothing.

Those around Charlie new Sam came from the Military, Special Forces. And most knew those in Special Forces were not talkers, but rather doers instead. And maybe that's where he acquired such a bullish approach to things, but Charlie appreciated it. No one else he liked having around when the Army stationed him anywhere but home. Sam took his job seriously. With his uncompromising-type of attitude and his skills, rarely, if at all, did one pull anything over on him. And that's just how Charlie liked it. Being home as little as he had been and with Sam for security made it somewhat easier for him when he returned to duty. Sure, he managed to reside for the most part quite a bit at the ranch while on duty, but when he toured overseas in his earlier years, knowing Sam and Lucia to be in his employment helped tamp down any extra worries. The two were professionals. They knew how to do their job. And proof gleaned like tumbleweeds in the pasture with proof of no other incident since the dreaded birthday party.

Cool and collect, Sam assessed the situation around them. He remained quiet until his scan of the area ended. After a long second, he reached for the door and opened it. In a low determined voice, he finally spoke. "All seems to be quiet now, Colonel."

Not fully registering how Sam replied, he started to climb in. But then the tingles started. They ran up his spine, not sharp pine needle ones, but more like blades of grass — itchy blades of grass.

His brow furrowed as he stood back up. "Not quiet?"

Which in all reality he understood it had been anything but quiet. Not with the fire and no doubt Susan's wrath, but by Sam's tone, he seemed to imply more.

"Explain."

Sam held the heavy door. "Mrs. Stockton requested I keep close watch over your daughter."

Charlie nodded. "Sounds like her."

And Charlie probably would have requested the same thing. Maybe, not this long, but at least for a day or two. Right?

A Cessna CJ2 flew down the runway with its landing gear ready for touchdown.

Charlie followed its path until it slowed at the end. "Did you have any problems?"

"She strongly requested I keep her out of Whiskey."

Sam examined the airstrip.

Charlie's gaze followed his.

The Cessna taxied toward the hanger on the other side of the airports offices. He waited for Sam to speak. But he said nothing.

Tension started to build in Charlie's neck. The muscles grew tighter. He took in a breath then slowly let it out. "Okay, Sam what aren't you telling me."

Sam pushed up on his aviators. "I've been asked not to talk about this, but I think you should know."

Charlie ran a hand through his hair then looked over at the helicopter. Thoughts of hopping back into the Bell tempted him. Not sure if he wanted Sam to continue, he weighed his choices.

Figure out what in blazes is going on with Evie, Susan, and that rotten clown or fly off for the horizon.

At that moment, his heart gave a little kick — just a reminder, that he promised Susan, if he ever headed for the horizon he'd take her with him. A flash of him setting the Bell onto a white sandy beach with Susan climbing out to walk in the surf with him on a desert island danced in front of him. Well, it did until the limo door squeaked with Sam's attempt to pull him back to their conversation without words.

Charlie laughed to himself causing his thoughts to fade. His gaze returned back to Sam once they all cleared.

Sam resembled a bull and sometimes had the temperament of one or at least that's what Evie complained about. So with his hesitancy, did Evie finally best him?

Now to most people on the ranch that would be an event to see. Not much riled Sam, but if anyone might get close, he knew Evie had the best shot. Although she carried a great sweetness in her personality and rivaled many great humanitarians, her stubbornness equaled no other. Well, all, but her mama's.

Not to chuckle at his employee, Charlie coughed into his hand as he turned to lean on the roof of the limo. Once the humor faded, he pulled down his sunglasses and stuffed them into his breast pocket. "Okay. Tell me."

Sam cleared his throat. "I understand Mrs. Stockton did not want me to take Ms. Evie back to Whiskey, but —"

Charlie's head snapped back to Sam. "But what?"

"Mrs. Stockton requested I drive both she and Ms. Evie to a lawyer's office in Whiskey."

A knot grew in Charlie's stomach. He placed a boot on the edge of the doorframe. His mind started to race. He only knew of one lawyer, but he never retained the man. And the lawyer's clients were small potatoes so Susan would not have him on retainer and especially not a lawyer from Whiskey. But for some reason he could not get a handle on it. A familiarity circled his thoughts about a meeting he entertained with Josiah — his brother-in-law. The meeting took place in the distant past, some twenty years ago. Charlie looked out over the top of the limo. No airfield stared back at him. Only the faintest image of Josiah and this lawyer.

Charlie's stomach rolled. He pulled off his Stetson and tossed it into the car. Maybe with a little more oomph than he planned as the hat now lay upside down against the other door. He blew out his breath. "Do you know what lawyer?"

Sam nodded once. "Mr. John Baxter."

Hmm? John Baxter.

The name had sounded familiar, but Charlie could not place it with any distinction. And especially not with Josiah. And why would he? After all, when he met with Josiah and his lawyer friend, he'd been home for leave around the holidays. And at that time in his life, his job in the military took precedence, not some stranger he'd met in passing. But, he would admit to at least himself, the thought of Susan and Evie meeting up with a lawyer worried him. And it especially worried him that Susan had not told him about any of it. As a last ditch resort and in desperate hope that it had nothing to do with Josiah, his mind raced over legal matters such as contracts he had for the Stockyard, but no John Baxter came into focus. The need for more info gnawed on his thoughts. And since Sam obviously thought it important, he know, he felt obligated to unburden him.

"Don't suppose you heard anything pertaining to the meeting?"

Sam adjusted his stance. "I noticed they argued for most of the trip home."

"On what?"

"Mr. Westerfield's shelter."

Charlie's gut dropped. He wiped at his forehead then glanced at his watch. "We better get going."

Sam nodded. "Yes, Sir."

With one foot in the car, Charlie ducked to climb in the rest of the way. "Anything else?"

Sam slowly closed the door. "Mr. Westerfield's shelter seemed to be the topic of discussion."

Charlie fell lopsided into his seat.

"The shelter?"

The door closed.

Charlie lay frozen in place. Josiah's name bounced around in his head, but stuck to nothing of recent. Even the shelter took a turn bouncing amongst his thoughts. Nothing worthwhile blossomed. But something stirred in his thoughts to remember.

Sam slid in behind the driver's wheel. "Where to Sir?"

Charlie pushed himself up and rubbed at the ache in his neck. He shifted in his seat. "You hear anything else on that drive?"

Sam turned to stare out the driver's window then after a minute caught Charlie's eyes in the rear view mirror. "Did the misses tell you her brother has been declared dead?"

Charlie rocked back into the leather seat of the limo. He rubbed a hand over his jaw. A conversation from a year ago broke free from the back of his head.

Sam turned the key.

The limo came to life.

A melody of Hank Williams played in the background.

"How long since Mr. Westerfield came up missing?"

Charlie looked toward the driver.

The memory of an argument between him and Susan stood right in front of him now.

'So what are you planning to do, pronounce him dead?'

Charlie's head fell back against the headrest. "Oh hell. That's what she did."

"Sir?"

Charlie shook his head as he straightened his Stetson on the seat next to him. "Never mind Sam. Take me to the ranch."

Sam agreed silently with a nod then threw the limo into drive.

Charlie pushed on the button to close the privacy partition. Unfortunately, the thoughts racing in his head remained, but grew louder.

Now what? And why all the sudden this lawyer? And Josiah? What in blazes did he do?

Charlie glanced out the window. The Texas sun sat almost high noon. The landscape slid past him without much notice. The private airfield he used lay on the outskirts of halfway between the ranch and San Antonio. If he went to the ranch, it would take about twenty minutes to get there. Then he would have to wait for the girls to get home. But if he went to the Foundation, he'd only have to wait the twenty-minute drive.

He cracked the partition and leaned forward.

"Sam?"

"Yes, Sir?"

"Change of plans."

"Sir?"

"Take me to the Foundation instead."

Sam nodded. "Yes, Sir."

The partition slid back up.

Charlie hit the lock switch then unbuttoned the collar of his dress shirt and loosened the bolero he wore instead of a silk tie.

Once again, he rubbed at the stiffness in the back of his neck. He closed his eyes and sank back into the leather seat. He took in a few deep breaths and let them out slowly.

Okay. This explains a lot.

He patted at his coat pockets. Once he hit the familiar object, he reached in and pulled out his phone. He stared at it for a minute. He contemplated calling both women, but then again thought better of it.

Right now with the frustration he felt toward both, he understood if he called Susan, they would argue and he didn't want that. Not after what she'd gone and done. And calling Evie would probably amount into an argument.

Better off texting Susan and surprising Evie.

He glanced at the clock app. "Okay, son, you got fifteen minutes. Get it done."

**

Charlie:	Darlin', I'm back. Be there shortly.
Susan:	Thank the Lord.
Charlie:	Susan?
Susan:	Your daughter is being impossible.
Charlie:	What happened?
Susan:	I'll deal with it.
Charlie:	Hopefully not the way you dealt with Josiah. Right?
Susan:	You know, husband's come up missing all the time too.
Charlie:	See you in a few.
Susan:	Good. We are breaking for lunch.
Charlie:	Where would you like to eat?
Susan:	Any place that has a good glass of red wine.
Charlie:	Starting a little early today?
Susan:	Starting?
Charlie:	Don't worry I'll handle this.
Susan:	Like I said make sure they have a cellar of good red wine.
Charlie:	Now it's a cellar?
Susan:	Okay. Fine. Make it a full bottle. A GOOD RED WINE.
Charlie:	Good?
Susan:	Changed my mind. Make it FABULOUS.
Charlie:	Only the best red for you, Darlin.

Chapter 4 Whiskey Tingles

THE TINGLES ON THE BACK OF CHARLIE'S NECK RETURNED. Not entirely sure what to make of it, he decided to delay any immediate action for its cause. The room he waited in belonged to Evie, more accurately her office at Mae Foundation. The room sat quiet with its traditional executive desk and chair with computer and paperwork piled on top with a small sitting area one might sit down at to get away for a moment or two of the stress. One could get quite comfy with the overstuffed couch and sleek club chairs with the faint classical notes of Mozart playing from some kind of hidden speaker system. Charlie sat back and closed his eyes in hopes if he relaxed the tingles would disappear. But not today.

When he walked through the Foundation's front doors, the company buzzed with energy. Not sure if it were good energy or bad energy, he decided to hunker down on one of the club chairs to stay out of the way. At first, he thought the energy a good high energy with most of the company working on all aspects of the present campaign. And he'd seen in the past how excited the staff got when working on a new campaign.

Charlie's gaze fell onto a wall of boards. Boards that displayed past, present, and future Mae Foundation. He stared at the middle board. It displayed the name Million Dollar Lady. He knew from conversations with Susan this board entertained the current campaign. In the middle, Evie must have pinned the face of this campaign. He smiled as he recognized the starlet's profile. In fact, he knew it well, after all, why would he not? The face that would launch this campaign would be none other than his wife's favorite actress. Elizabeth Garner. As he studied the boards, he noticed what looked to be a discarded one propped against the trashcan. He frowned as he recognized its name — All American Girl. He shook his head. "That's not good."

He knew from his daughter's updates she'd worked hard on putting that one together and then with one swift text message, she'd scrapped the whole campaign.

The tingles intensified.

Ever since he walked into the Foundation that afternoon, the air sizzled with energy. Most would think a high positive energy, after all, they were filming for the new campaign, but not to Charlie. No instead negative energy surrounded him. And lots of it. Not many times did his neck hairs stand at attention, but today they did. So when the hall outside quieted as if those in it waited for a storm to pass, Charlie sat up and waited for the hit.

And as if on cue, the office door flew open — the hit. The calm vanished only to have its void replaced by a more negative one.

Charlie scooted to the edge of the club seat readying to stand when his daughter, Evie stomped through the door heading straight for the refrigerator.

The tall, young auburn-haired woman resembled a younger version of his wife. She marched directly for the target without assessing her surroundings first.

With a lopsided grin growing on his face, he inched his way to the edge of his seat.

He studied his daughter.

She halted at the refrigerator, yanked open the door, white knuckled a water bottle, and crack the seal on it.

Not spotting Charlie, he chuckled to himself when she shotgunned the bottle of water she cracked open. After one long drink, she slammed the plastic bottle on top of her desk. A geyser of water spewed through the opening.

Evie growled.

Charlie laughed to himself. He recognized the frustration in his daughter's actions. And from what he had learned over the past few days, the frustration had only one source — her mamma.

He tipped back his hat with his index finger ready to lend some advice, but Evie pulled out her phone at the last minute and stabbed at the screen.

Charlie frowned. He said nothing and instead waited on the edge of his seat. Ready to stand, he hoped his daughter would finally notice him.

She did not.

he cleared his throat — nothing.

The hint of a smile tugged at his lips. Not wanting to disrespect his daughter's frustration, he waited. But the more he watched her pound on the screen of her phone, the harder it became to contain the chuckle building. After all, he understood Evie's frustration when it came to her mamma. They married almost thirty-five years ago so he had plenty of experience with how she dealt with things. And one thing he learned over the past years, if Susan felt loss, her control would only grow stronger. And with the loss of her only brother seven years ago and the declaration of his death, her grip on holding her family together had grown tight like a vice. And now, he could see the sparks of manipulation flaring over Evie. He glanced back over at the discarded campaign.

Charlie shook his head at one final attempt to shake off the chuckle. Unfortunately, though with every stab she made, it only made it harder for him. And with the last stab of her fingernail to the screen, the chuckle broke free.

Evie squeaked.

Charlie tipped back his hat and smiled as he watched Evie spin in his direction.

She rocked to a stop. Her shoulders fell.

Charlie stood. His grin grew to the size of Texas. "Darlin' when you act like that, you remind me so much of your mamma."

Evie rolled her eyes and tacked her hands to her hips. "Daddy, sorry, but you're way off on that one."

Now standing, Charlie removed his rich chocolatey Stetson and slapped it against his thigh. "Evie, you might not see it, but you're the spitting image of your Mama."

"Ha! I don't think so."

Charlie crossed the floor and swooped Evie up into a big hug. "Business is finished in Austin. I'm back home now."

Evie stared up at him. Her brow furrowed. "Does Mama know?"

Charlie smiled down at her. "She does. And I'm here to take the two most beautiful women to lunch."

Evie snorted. "Right. This beautiful girl isn't going anywhere."

Charlie growled on the inside. His old days of barking out orders stirred within him. But he understood these two women in his life were no soldiers and he no longer commanded anyone or anything, but maybe his cattle, so whenever he fell into a rut of what to do he did the only thing a good officer would do. Call on a higher power for help. And he did. He closed his eyes and tilted his chin upwards.

Lord, going to need your help on this one. Please give me the strength to deal with these two and make both of them happy.

Evie shifted in his arms.

Charlie lifted Evie's chin. One of his eyebrows arched. "You sure about that?"

Text Message
April 23rd
12:07 PM

Charlie: Darlin', you ready for lunch?

Susan: No!

Charlie: Problems?

Susan: Problems???

Charlie: Should I even ask?

Susan: Are you being rhetorical?

Charlie: Maybe.

Susan: Wow! Nice to know you care.

Charlie: Do we need to postpone lunch?

Susan: Where are you?

Charlie: Waiting for you.

Susan: Where?

Charlie: Outside.

Susan: Outside? Outside in the lobby? Or outside in the limo?

Charlie: Limo.

Susan: Why?

Charlie: I've always had a fantasy of whisking you away for lunch on my horse.

Susan: But the limo's no horse.

Charlie: Go with me on this, Darlin'.

Susan: Would love to, but I've got flames to put out here.

Charlie: So, no lunch?

Susan: Can you wait?

Charlie: For you? Always.

Susan: Good. Need to discuss campaign changes with Evie.

Charlie: So this is more like dinner then?

Susan: If directions are followed, then no.

Charlie: Hahaha!

Susan: Charles, you know you could support me on this.

Charlie: I could.

Susan: Good to know. Will see you in twenty minutes.

Charlie: Anything else?

Susan: Call ahead to Le Café de Bistro and reserve a table for two.

Charles: Anything else?

Susan: Order ahead a bottle of their best red, slightly chilled.

Charlie: A bottle?

Susan: Add a second to be safe.

Charlie: One is enough, But if you'd prefer coffee instead, I'd support two then.

Susan: I'll be out soon.

Charlie: Just curious. You wearing heels or boots?

Susan: Heels. Why?

Charlie: Just a needed detail.

Susan: Detail? For what?

Charlie: A fantasy.

Susan: Fantasy?

Charlie: What color?

Susan: Charles!

Charlie: Let's just say you've been missed.

Susan: Really? You've been gone a lot longer.

Charlie: An old cowboy told me I've been a fool.

Susan: A fool? What old cowboy told you this?

Charlie: Me.

Susan: Aw!

Charlie: One bottle of the best red slightly chilled coming up.

Susan: And Charlie…Their RED!

Charlie: Holy smokes! Two it is.

<h1 style="text-align:center">Chapter 5 Whiskey Riverwalk</h1>

RED WINE NEVER QUENCHED CHARLIE'S THIRST. In fact, he would never drink it, but being that Susan loved the stomped grapes, He ordered the finest the bistro had on hand. If she had never requested it, Charlie probably would have ordered a whiskey, but better yet a good hardy cup of coffee. And since Susan felt she needed a glass even though she really wanted a bottle or two, Charlie thought best not to indulge her since she had to deal with all the stressors regarding the fire and her latest campaign.

Not too uncomfortable with the quaint setting even though he preferred one of his fabulous steak houses, he would enjoy it as long as he dined with his wife. He'd missed out on many meals with her and his daughter and now with his retirement, he planned on not missing any more.

Charlie glanced around. He honestly could not remember if he and Susan had patronized the place before, but they must have. Everyone seemed to know them. And now out on the patio, he sat at a prime location. The view couldn't have been any better.

Two wine goblets sat on the white linen tablecloth. Silverware lay wrapped in a smaller piece of the fabric. A small plate of goat cheese and crackers sat between the weaved placemats. The soft notes of a Mozart concerto streamed out from hidden speakers near the corners of the overhead panels of trellis with ivy and miniature yellow roses dangling down. A sparse amount of patrons filled the outside café tables. Only the outer rim were occupied and rightly so, with the gorgeous view of the Riverwalk, which ran alongside the San Antonio river. Most of the crowd would just now break for lunch if the shops and entertainment along the river didn't distract them.

Charlie leaned back in his chair and studied the people as they passed. They ranged from joggers, shoppers, and even a pair of kayakers strolled by.

One of Charlie's eyebrows arched at the site of a young girl who looked a lot like Evie. She had a darker shorter version of auburn hair, but same tall toned build. He watched as she struggled with a sandwich board sign advertising the latest show over in the theater section of the Riverwalk. A smile came to his face as the girl and her sandwich board reminded him of something Evie might do just to help out a struggling business. That would infuriate her mamma.

A young man cleared his voice as he approached the table. With black slacks on and a crisp white button-up shirt, he stopped next to Charlie. "Colonel, would you care for another glass?"

Charlie turned to examine the glasses. The one closest to him, he figured had a sip or two drank from it, but the other one, well it had maybe a swallow or two left. He then glanced at the plate of cheese and crackers. A good-sized dent in the appetizer seemed missing. He smiled to himself. Before he answered the waiter, he looked past the tables closest to the patio's entrance and saw Susan talking to another couple.

His belly grumbled, he wanted to order more, but paused. The thought of what Susan would want rolled around in his head like a tumbleweed. He glanced back at the wine goblets.

The waiter teetered on his heels.

Charlie sighed.

Indecision surfaced as his brow furrowed. Charlie had no clue as whether or not to order another glass for Susan. Sure, she mentioned getting a bottle or two to drink due to the stress she dealt with, but did she really mean it? And as for the meal would he choose the right dish?

Charlie fingered the stem of her glass. Lipstick stuck to the edge. A light peach frost, a color that looked absolutely stunning against her milky skin and auburn hair. Charlie swiveled in his seat as he picked up the glass. He held it up and jiggled the contents as if signaling to its wayward consumer. His lips quirked to one side as the thought of letting a low whistle call to his wife tempted him, but lucky for Susan, she looked in his direction. The quirk of her head and the impish smile that appeared gave Charlie the okay to order more wine and their meals.

Charlie nodded at the waiter who pulled out some sort of electronic ordering device.

"Sir?"

Charlie stretched his neck to catch a glimpse of the sidewalk board announcing the daily special, which if he made out the chalk writing, he just ordered he and Susan the salmon entree with asparagus and a side salad, plus more wine.

The waiter tapped the device's screen. "Thank you, Sir. I'll be back with more wine."

On that cue, Charlie reached for his glass and just as it touched his lips, Susan returned. Not forgetting his manners, he set down his goblet, pushed back his chair, and stood. He placed a hand on the small of his wife's back. Her warmth radiated into his hand through her black silk blouse with sprinkles of red throughout. The heat made him linger to pull out her chair. Charlie glanced over the rest of her body noticing her multi-pleated black slacks, and the clincher… the red heels. His heart thumped in approval. The corner of his mouth rose with his amazement how she managed to look radiant in a red that did not match her hair. But with its dark undertones, anything she wore with the color black in it seemed to negate the difference in reds.

And only when Susan laughed with a twinkle in her eyes did he help her sit. As he scooted her in, he leaned into her ear. "You were right about the red. It's an excellent choice."

Not pulling her head away, but actually leaning into Charlie, she let her eyes drift closed. "Thank you, I appreciate your confidence in my choice of wine."

Charlie inhaled the sweet notes of Susan's perfume. Heat stirred in his chest. He chuckled to himself as he returned to his seat. "Darlin', I just hope my selection for lunch is as worthy."

"I'm sure I will love it."

And with those words, the tingles that always appeared when some cosmic force stirred to change the mood hit. Sometimes they were good tingles, but most of the time not so good. The tingles he got started as a youngster, but he could not recall such prominent ones until he signed up for the Army. He always figured them as his sixth sense. Many times when he found himself in a bad situation, he noticed the spiky tingles just before something hit. And when that something hit, for the most part if not more like always, it hit bad. Luckily, for him though, he recognized this as a signal to watch out, a surprise, whether it be good or bad, he knew to expect something. But to be honest, these tingles attacking his neck were not the usual spiky ones. Not able to put a finger on them, he however understood that they were different.

Hmm?

Had it been her words or the somewhat carefree attitude. But before he could figure out which, Susan drug one of her manicured fingers over the top of his hand.

Caught off guard from her touch, the thoughts Charlie contemplated disappeared.

Susan's manicured finger moved in a circular motion on the top of his hand. The sensation felt good on his calloused hand. Her soft fingertip with the edginess of her nail sparked a whole new sensation. Her touch always mesmerized him. In fact, the world around them faded away except for the kick of his heart.

The feelings that emanated from her touch went to every good nerve ending he had. From every drag and swirl of her finger, Charlie lost himself in her touch. He'd missed this playfulness of his wife.

Sure, he retired a while back, but the closeness had been missing for a good part of the time he'd been in the Service. Yes, they'd had their time together when on leave, but in his own thoughts, it never seemed long enough for them to get back into that comfortable ease one has when they spent day and night with their spouse. And it had to be a long period of time— like maybe thirty years or so.

On that thought, hope pushed in on his thoughts.

The curl of Charlie's lips went higher. Maybe things were starting to come around like a normal couple who got to live day and night with their spouse. And come to think of it, he'd been home a year now without leaving her behind.

Well, almost a year.

Charlie groaned on the inside when the notion of him being gone for the last week hit him.

You idiot. Stop doing that. No more ventures out for more than a day without her.

Charlie opened his eyes and took in his wife. She continued to circle his hand with her manicured fingernail all while she spoke about something. Charlie cringed when he realized he had no idea of what Susan had said or even what she said now.

A twitch of those spikes just waiting in the background poked at his neck. But Charlie mentally brushed them off.

Not today fellas.

He made a silent vow that from now on when Susan touched him, he'd make sure to listen and not get carried away with how good her touch felt.

Yeah. Sure. Right.

And in response to his newest vow, the tap dance his heart did against his ribs slowed.

The sounds around Charlie slowly came back to him. The clank of dishware being gathered up from another table, low murmurs from other guests, and the noise off the Riverwalk grew. Susan's voice finally broke through the affect her touch had on him. "Charles, the couple I just spoke to are supporters of my Million Dollar Lady campaign, which is helping to fund the local Humane Society."

He nodded. "And?"

Susan cocked an eyebrow. "Excuse me?"

Before Charlie answered, he drug his tongue over his teeth making sure to get the last bit of cracker and goat cheese — A stalling technique he liked to use so to map out in his head how to proceed. After all, the mention of her Million Dollar Lady campaign, the one that occupied all of her time had some problems from what she'd mentioned to him over the past few weeks. And most of those problems leaned toward Evie's doing or at least from Susan's point of view.

"That's interesting. Have they done anything to promote both of them?"

Susan picked up her goblet and took a sip while her other hand continued to move over his. "They have been actively researching a few things down here on the Riverwalk."

The waiter returned with a bottle of the red. "Ma'am would you care for more?"

Susan held up her glass. "Please."

The wine plunged into the deep goblet and filled the glass to the rim.

She smiled up at the waiter. "Thank you."

He smiled back and nodded. Then pivoting he offered the bottle to Charlie. "Sir?"

But before Charlie agreed to the refill, the robust scent of coffee drifted past him as another waiter passed by their table with a carafe of coffee and two cups.

He breathed deep allowing the aroma to saturate each pore in his body. But not to add to the bill or ruin the mood, because he knew Susan would not approve especially since she had wanted the red wine. He tilted his head toward his wine glass. "Top it off. I'll be fine then."

The waiter smiled. "Yes, Sir."

While the waiter tended to the wine, Charlie went back to studying his wife. His heart thumped hard once again reminding him what he'd missed for the past thirty plus years.

Thirty years of this, you missed out on. You, Colonel are a stupid, stupid man.

The touch of her finger grew a little rougher. Charlie jerked his attention back to the conversation.

"Sorry, I was just reminding myself on what I've missed for all these years."

Susan's back stiffened. She pulled her hand away. Her gaze narrowed on him. "Excuse me?"

Even though the Texas sun hung high overhead and it's rays streamed through the overhead trellis like gold ribbons, the warmth vanished from Charlie's hand. His brow furrowed. "Darlin'?"

Susan picked up her wine glass. She lifted it to her mouth, but before she took a drink, she set it back down. "Didn't you hear anything I said?"

Charlie picked up his glass and took a long drink. When he set it down his gaze roamed the patio searching for the waiter, better yet the wine bottle.

"Charles?"

On the obvious warning tone, Charlie nodded with a grin. "I sure did."

Not able to cross his fingers for the lie, Charlie mentally did it. He had the notion to tell her he had been lost in his thoughts regarding her and how stupid he'd been for the last thirty years chasing after a dream of becoming a general when he probably realized he'd never get that rank ten years ago. But informing Susan of this would probably not be one of his best moves. So instead, he stretched the truth.

"Now Darlin', I heard every word you said."

Susan smiled. Her eyes danced.

And the tingles shot into Charlie's neck like barbed wire. He cringed on the inside.

Oh, Lord. What did I just do.

Susan laughed. "So you don't mind the colors we did the kitchen in?"

Charlie gulped. "No ma'am. I'm sure they look beautiful."

Susan's eyes danced. "And the smokiness won't bother you?"

Charlie shook his head while he picked up her hand and pulled it toward his lips. "No, Ma'am, it can't be any worse than gunpowder."

The prickles in Charlie's neck intensified almost to the point he might need something stronger than wine. But he would not let on that he had not heard a word she said. But if all he missed were Susan's concerns of him minding on how she renovated the kitchen and that there might be a lingering smokey smell then he might get out of this without looking like a jackass.

Another sharp twinge pierced Charlie's neck. A few words of displeasure passed underneath his breath.

Susan must have noticed the tightness in his jaw and the discomfort that oozed past his lips. Her smile widened.

The clench of his teeth must have given him away.

"Oh Charlie, I'm so glad you will talk to Evie about her responsibility to Mae Foundation. I mean, when I heard she wanted to leave to go open that shelter, she's not thinking about her responsibilities as the chief marketing executive. But we know Evie wouldn't do such a thing, right?"

Charlie's eyebrows rose.

What?

" I just couldn't believe it. My assistant Mary, must be wrong. And you know how rumors spread quickly when someone thinks someone else isn't happy. Right?"

Charlie stared blankly at Susan as the words stampeded through his head.

Evie wants to quit? Run the shelter? She's unhappy? Her responsibilities? Rumors? What in the world is going on?

Susan squeezed Charlie's fingers. "And how important it is that she work harder with her responsibilities."

Charlie's gut sank. He swore to himself. He eyed Susan wearily. Almost positive he didn't agree to anything of the sort, he now had to either admit he hadn't heard the first part of their conversation, which in turn made him out as a liar or he would have to go with the flow and somehow get Susan to back off and let Evie find her own way. Either way, he needed to get ready for battle.

Charlie put his warrior face on. He smiled, but not just any old smile, no this one pulled at the corner of one side of his lips. His eyes darkened as they danced. He lifted Susan's hand and before he placed a kiss on her creamy skin he leaned forward for her ears only. "Yes, Darlin'. In fact, I'll set things right with her."

Susan's face lit up. "Oh Charlie," she cradled her hands around his jaw. "You're wonderful. I knew I could depend on you."

Charlie held back the scream he wanted to let out when Susan's nails caressed his jaw. The heat that sored over his skin did not come from the heat her touch generated earlier. No, this time, it came from barbed-like twinges that danced like a ring of fire around his neck.

Even though Charlie hadn't really committed to helping Susan with Evie, he hadn't said he wouldn't either. First, he needed to scout out the whole matter to assess the battlefield, because yes, this would end up in some kind of skirmish and not wanting to choose sides at the moment, Charlie did the only thing he could. He'd act like Switzerland and be neutral. He groaned on the inside knowing neither women would appreciate the gesture. But for now, until he got more details, he refused to pick sides.

Susan pressed her lips softly into his.

Charlie knew he should stop the kiss, but he could never resist her. And frankly, he didn't want to either. After all, Susan knew him and he had the feeling she knew she caught him not listening, so he'd go along with her tactics and eventually make up his own mind. But in the meantime, his wife wanted the kiss, so he would oblige her.

He deepened the kiss as his heart kicked out an S.O.S.

Text Message
April 24
6:10 AM

Charlie: Good morning, Sunshine!

Evie: Daddy?

Charlie: Yep!

Evie: Its 6:15 in the morning. You alright?

Charlie: Sure am. How about you?

Evie: Tired. Can I go back to sleep now?

Charlie: Not till you tell me what's going on.

Evie: With what?

Charlie: Your Mamma.

Evie: Oh, that. Sure.

Charlie: Well?

Evie: Where should I start?

Charlie: How about with the rumor.

Evie: What rumor?

Charlie: The rumor that you might be quitting.

Evie: Sorry. Not a rumor.

Charlie: Is it that bad there?

Evie: Yep. I'm the CMO and Mother overrides my decisions all the time.

Charlie: Have you talked to her? I mean really talk to her?

Evie: I've tried, but she won't listen. You know how she gets.

Charlie: Hmm? Sounds like someone else I know.

Evie: Honestly, Daddy, I've tried. Guess my heart isn't in it.

Charlie: I saw this coming years ago.

Evie: You did?

Charlie: Yes. When you worked for Josiah. I knew you found your calling.

Evie: Why didn't you say anything then?

Charlie: Why didn't you?

Evie: Guess I didn't want to disappoint Mother.

Charlie: Just talk to her.

Evie: Okay. I'll try.

Charlie: Good girl! Just make sure this is what you want.

Chapter 6 Whiskey Resignation

A TRAIL OF DIRT AND STRAW LAY ON THE FLOOR. Charlie berated himself for not pulling off his boots first when he came into the house, but at the moment, his stomach vetoed that whole process in an attempt to get lunch and a coffee. As he looked back over the floor he just traveled, he figured he would clean up the mess himself if he had to. After all, he made it, he would clean it up. It would not be the first time to do such a thing. He hated it when people didn't clean up their own messes or in the least apologize for it and compensate the one who did clean it up. He nodded to himself. It wouldn't be any trouble, he'd just get a broom. Nevertheless, he worked with the ranch hands getting the last few calves branded since before the rooster crowed and he'd be the first to admit that the cup of coffee and toast he had at breakfast didn't fill him up. He shook his head at those foolish thoughts. And now, that the last of his heard received their Stockyard brand, he decided before the ranch hands revolted to call it quits for lunch. He made a mental note to clean it up himself or ask their housekeeper for help with the mess right after he ate some food. The image of a roast beef sandwich and some chips and homemade salsa made his stomach grumble. The scent of a strong rich roast of coffee drifted from the kitchen. Charlie licked his lips He took in a deep breath. Not wanting to delay the reality of lunch, he pivoted in his dirt-tarnished boots to enter the dining room, but halted.

What the—

Charlie's hunger pulled back when it registered he would not be eating alone today.

At first, his face started to light up, but then as this guest registered his brows furrowed. The confusion surfacing didn't come from the person per say, but instead because why they were here in the first place did. Normally, his lunch guest didn't have time. Normally, he'd spend it alone most days. Normally, his guest ate at the office or at some fancy bistro or café along the Riverwalk.

He rubbed at his jaw.

Now what brings her home for lunch today?

Charlie moved from foot to foot not sure what to do. Usually, it meant trouble brewing and at the moment, Charlie only wanted one thing, well actually two — a cup of freshly brewed coffee and lunch.

The surprise stopped his thoughts on what he needed to do for the rest of the day. And instead, his thoughts now wondered why of all days he'd be eating lunch with his wife.

Usually when Susan came home for lunch it meant something troubled her and she readied to do battle. His heart poked at him and told him he had it all wrong. Maybe she just wanted to have lunch with her husband. You know, you.

Charlie shook his head. He didn't buy that scenario. He studied her from behind another minute. And only when her back straightened like a board and her head turned away from the San Antonio Express business section did he realize she sensed him behind her.

Now or never. Dinner's a long way off from now.

Charlie glanced at his boots and clothes. The boots were still somewhat muddy and his pants had a bit of dust on them, but for the most part, he could sit down and eat without much complaint from his wife. And hay, maybe she'd surprise him and not mention his appearance. In any case, she must have had something else on her mind, if she'd taken the time to come home for lunch. She must have something important to discuss, right?

Charlie nodded and with a wave of his hands over his jeans, his mood went from a troubled to a cheery one as the dust vanished from the front of his jeans.

Remember cowboy, it's not often you get to eat lunch with your bride. You got thirty plus years to make up to her.

Charlie stepped into the dining room.

Susan lowered the San Antonio Express. "Is it true Charles? Did Evie do it?"

Charlie placed a hand on the back of her chair and leaned toward her. "Evie? Resigned?" He cocked his head. An image of him standing in Evie's office the other day played across his brain. His overhearing her talking to her friend, Margo about the shelter and his text message with her this morning played at the back of his memories. He swore to himself. "I reckon it might be."

He bent his tall lean frame over and brushed his lips across her cheek.

Susan's face fell. Disappointment flashed in her eyes.

Charlie's gut tightened. Not knowing what to do, he did the one thing that might possibly distract Susan from doing or saying anything foolish. He leaned in and brushed his lips across hers.

"Charles, please." She pushed on him. "My makeup."

"Woah now." Charlie didn't budge. But instead, he cradled his wife's chin in his callused hands. He studied her. He could sense the anger boiling inside her with her jaw clenched and her eyes dancing in a war pattern. If he wanted to have a civil conversation over lunch, he would need to do something to tamper it down.

Charlie leaned down almost a whisper breath between their lips. "Darlin'." He caressed her skin with his thumbs.

Susan's eyes closed. Her chin lifted. A reluctant sigh escaped from her tawny –glazed lips.

An ornery grin tugged at one side of Charlie's mouth.

The room heated up. Charlie so wanted to lean in with a kiss, but he knew it would not end there. Heck lunch would not happen and they would probably never get anything resolved with regards to Evie. So best thing to do until he got a better handle on whether or not Evie resigned would be if he got her thinking about something else. Well, no not just thinking, more like mad and thinking. Charlie cringed on the inside knowing full well he played dirty, but as the Military had trained them, when it came to winning a battle all tactics were fair as long as you came out the winner… for the most part. Now Susan might not think so, but he'd deal with that later.

His lips brushed hers. Susan licked her bottom lip. The pulse in her neck raced.

Charlie groaned to himself

Lord help me.

"Darlin' don't worry. If it's true, we'll figure it out. But —"

Susan's eyes flew open. Her head pulled from his hands. She growled. "Charles. How dare you."

Charlie shook his head. The quirk of a grin held on. He side stepped to his chair and pulled it out to sit. He grabbed for the linen napkin next to his plate and shook it out. Laying it across his lap, he lifted his head. "Sorry Darlin'. And don't worry you look radiant."

The business section of the newspaper crumbled under his wife's French manicured fingers. Her face-hardened. "Don't you dare play these games with me. This is important."

Charlie hung his head. But not because Susan figured out his little game to distract her, but because he had lots to do today on the ranch. And now it looked as if he'd have this thrown onto his plate to deal with. And speaking of plates, lunch would now probably turn into something indigestible if he got any at all. He clenched his fists bracing for the fight.

Susan narrowed her gaze at him and pointed with a knife. "Did Sam know?"

"Who?"

"Sam."

Charlie rubbed the grizzled shadow forming on his face. "Sam's her driver. Why would he know?"

"That's really hard to believe. The man drives her everywhere. It's hard to believe he didn't hear her mention it to anyone. Are you sure we can trust him?"

Charlie's eyes constricted. His fist tightened. "Trust him? Trust Sam? Are you serious?"

The question infuriated Charlie. How could he not trust Sam? The man had worked for them since Evie's kidnapping. Nothing like that day had ever happened to Evie or Susan since Charlie hired the ex-special forces soldier. Charlie understood those guys had a code and to them they kept that code all their life. And when they agreed to protect and serve then they did even if it meant giving up on their own life. And for this dedication that Sam gave to him in protecting this wife and daughter created a bond between them — all of them. SO how Susan could ask such a thing, just about blew his mind apart.

Charlie glared at his wife until what seemed like a tumbleweed rolled across the pasture broke the spell of anger. The Stockton's forty-something year old housekeeper entered the room carrying a carafe of coffee.

"*Perdoñ, Señor, Señora* coffee?"

The tension eased.

Susan grimaced. "No Lucia. I'll just have lemon water and a salad. Coffee will do nothing but make my stomach worse."

"*Sí, Señora.*"

Lucia stepped up to the table. "Señor?"

Charlie held out his cup.

"I'm not happy either. If she wanted time off I'm, sure we could have arranged something. And as for Sam. Don't try to blame him for this."

Lucia held up the small silver carafe with wide eyes, but didn't pour the coffee. "*Señor?*"

Charles arched a gray eyebrow at his empty cup. "Lucia?"

"Did *Señorita* Evie leave?"

A crackle came from the newspaper. Susan held it crushed around her fingers. She huffed. "Yes, Lucia. But she'll return."

Charles nodded. "It looks that way."

Lucia bit her lip, and nodded. "*Sí Señor.*"

Susan tapped a finger on the table. "Lucia, our salads, please."

"*Ah, sí, un momento.*" The housekeeper hustled out of the room.

Susan leaned forward. "If she isn't back by the first of the week, you better call Humphry."

Charles eyebrows furrowed. He tipped the cup. Nothing splashed out. He frowned. "Coffee?"

Susan folded the paper and laid it next to her plate. "Charles?"

He put down the cup. "Is that necessary?"

Susan stiffened. "I'll take whatever steps I have to."

She brushed off a piece of lint on her designer suit. "I want her back here. She has a responsibility to the family. Her duty is to help run Mae Foundation. I won't accept anything less."

Charlie rolled his eyes as he set down his empty cup. Okay, fine. "I'll call Humphrey next Monday."

Lucia returned. She carried a full tray of salads and ice lemon water. She set the water down in front of Susan. Then she placed a plate of salad in front of each of them.

Charlie held up his cup.

Susan smiled waving her hand in dismissal. "Thank you Lucia."

Lucia rubbed a hand down her apron. "*Sí, Señora.*"

Charles gaze followed Lucia as she left the room. "But my —"

Susan snapped. "Charles, just eat your salad."

A crack of thunder shook the house.

Charlie Looked up. The chandelier lights flickered. He sighed and set down his cup. He grimaced at the salad. "Yes, Darlin'."

Charlie:	An e-mail? What happened to you two talking?
Evie:	Sorry. She refused to listen.
Charlie:	Storm's hit. Afraid it's going to be a big one.
Evie:	No rain yet here. Lots of thunder though.
Charlie:	You got that right.
Evie:	Daddy?
Charlie:	You know, it's not too late to come back.
Evie:	Oh! Sorry. I can't.
Charlie:	Is there nothing I can do to get you to stay?
Evie:	No. Sorry Daddy.
Charlie:	Okay. It might be rough at first.
Evie:	I know, but I'll manage.
Charlie:	Not you, me.
Evie:	LOL
Charlie:	You know your Mamma blames me, right?
Evie:	No. Only Uncle Josiah is to blame.
Charlie:	True. But don't want to open that can of worms.
Evie:	Thanks Daddy!
Charlie:	Don't thank me yet.
Evie:	Again. Sorry.
Charlie:	Don't be a stranger around here.
Evie:	Best to stay away a bit. You know, let Mother calm down.
Charlie:	You know we are talking about your Mamma, right?
Evie:	You could always come see me if things get too rough.
Charlie:	No worries. I've been through worse.
Evie:	Again, sorry, Daddy.
Charlie:	Long time since I bunked in the barn. If things worsen, look for me there.
Evie:	Trying to make me feel guilty?
Charlie:	Is it working?

Evie: Nope, sorry!
Charlie: Hmm? Stubborn just like your Mamma.
Evie: Love you, Daddy!
Charlie: Yep, just like your Mamma.

Chapter 7 Whiskey Truth

CHARLIE BENT USING HIS LEGS AND NOT HIS BACK. A gold nugget he picked up years ago and not one he'd discard any time soon. One might think of this nugget he picked up in the service, but he'd been born with rancher's blood and since he could pull on his first pair of cowboy boots one of his first jobs on the farm had been mucking out the stalls. And now well past retirement, he continued to muck out stalls. But mucking out stalls would rank first if he had to choose now. After all, hauling bodies out of war zones did build up muscles, but those who lent no assistance-wreaked havoc on his body physically from the dead weight, but more mentally. So any chance he got to muck out a stall in his barn he took it. In spite of everything, he'd rather deal with the manure and straw then the memories that would sometimes flood his brain at the drop of his hat.

He slid the tines of the pitchfork under the soiled straw and straightened to stand. But a vibration rattled his concentration. He looked down at his jeans. The hint of the outline of his phone pressed against his pant leg. The movement prickled his skin.

Charlie grunted as he dumped the contents and set the fork against the stall wall. He reached for his phone. The screen signaled an incoming video call. He scanned the floor. He still had half the stull to clean out. And at this rate with a phone call, yet alone it being a video call, he'd never get this chore done.

Yes, Charlie hired lots of hands to do the chores on the ranch, but he helped out with things like this. A good commander is never afraid to get in and do the dirty work himself. Shows the men he's in it with them and he'd never assign any duty he wouldn't do himself. He tipped back his Stetson and pulled the screen closer unsure of which button to activate the video call.

He blew out his breath and jabbed one finger on to what looked like a connect button. The screen changed and the image of a bottle of Barleyshot Whiskey — cinnamon whiskey to be exact filled the front of his phone.

Charlie licked his lips.

A deep voice rang out. "Charlie, you finally managed to answer or did you have to get one of the steers to do it for you?"

Charlie rolled his eyes. "Knew I should have never connected the barn up to Wi-Fi."

"What's that? Charlie, speak up."

"Jack, you old son of a gun. Glad you finally fitted me into your schedule. I feel honored."

Charlie grinned wide. "Or did your bride finally decide to get that annulment?"

A hardy chuckle rolled out from the phone's speaker. "No. She still believes she can reform me."

Charlie dipped his head. "Good girl."

"Yes, sir, that she is."

Charlie turned and walked over to the front of the stall. Putting the Phone up against the door where a slight edge stuck out, he rested it there then turned back and grabbed his pitchfork. He held it up for Jack to get a good view of it. "Afraid you caught me at a bad time."

"Bad time? Devil taking vacation?"

Charlie smiled. "No Sir. Trying to stay prepared. Figured you'd call sometime."

"Prepared? Prepared for what?"

Charlie smiled. "Reckoned I'd need to shovel some of your BS out of the way when we talked."

The cinnamon whiskey bottle left the screen. In place, Jack Barleyshot peered out from the screen. The cowboy wore a rugged grin on his tan face that the Texas sunshine never managed to forget to leave behind. He raised a silver eyebrow. A silver eyebrow that by no means compared to Charlie's at the moment. And in all reality, that left little in comparison for Charlie and Jack, or even the nearest minting facility.

"So you want to know what's going on in Whiskey, huh?"

Charlie nodded with the curl of one side of his mouth higher than the other. "I do. And I appreciate you returning the call. Even though it's been a week."

"How about you call that restaurant of yours and we talk over one of the Stockyard's juicy steaks. I'll even buy a bottle of Whiskey for an appetizer."

"I'd love to, but I need the info now. Not when you can clear that so-called schedule of yours. You know, some of us got others that depend on us."

Jack scoffed. "Okay. Now who's slinging the bull —"

Charlie laughed while he stood straightening his back. With one hand, he held up the pitchfork. "Okay, seriously. Jack, give me the lowdown on Whiskey."

"You want anything in particular?"

Charlie shook his head. He grabbed the pitchfork with both hands and scooped up another pile of manure and straw. "Got anything on Josiah's shelter?"

Nothing came from the phone. For a moment, Charlie thought he'd lost the connection and without having to look over his shoulder at the phone, Charlie figured Jack might be stalling. But why? Curiosity pulled at his brain, so instead of him waiting for Jack to pick up where he left off, he peeked over his shoulder.

The screen remained lit.

His friend said nothing.

A few mews of the cattle called out.

Not wanting to waste time, Charlie carried the pitchfork to the open stall door and tossed the contents into a waiting wheelbarrow. He heard the tinkle of a glass with ice cubes dropping into it and a splash of liquid crashing overtop the ice cubes. Then the metallic groan of a chair came from the phone. He watched his friend lean back. Jack pulled a rocks glass to his lips. A brown liquid with a red tinge to it filled the glass half way. Jack swirled it underneath his nose before he took a sniff. Then before Charlie could ask if he planned on drinking the whiskey or tormenting him, Jack raised it to his lips and swallowed.

Charlie licked his lips.

The ice in the glass clinked as Jack held it up and examined it. Less than two finger's worth remained. Jack grinned. "Only thing that would make this taste better would be one of those cigars."

"Cigars?"

"You know. Like the one we had just before we flew out for the assignment in Mogadishu."

Charlie smiled as the memory hit him. Jack always had a way of lightening the mood. And the mention of a night he, Jack and a few chopper pilots finished off a few bottles the night before their deadliest mission always made him realize what he went through now would never compare to those times. Basically, Jack wanted to remind him whatever problems he had now, would never measure up to those disastrous times in his past. So, in a roundabout way, Jack let him know he needed to lighten up. Things would resolve one way or another. Maybe not how he might expect it, but however it did, it would never get as bad as it had in Mogadishu. And like Mogadishu, he'd come out of it alive. Maybe a little banged up, but alive.

Charlie walked over to the phone and leaned closer. "New batch?"

Jack smiled. His eyes danced. "Yeh, believe it or not, we've had barrels worth of request for cinnamon whiskey. Thought we'd try and get some made for next Christmas."

"Any good?"

Jack cringed then his face lost some color. He shook his head. "Not sure on this one."

"Oh Yeh?"

Jack pounded his fist into the middle of his sternum. "Yeh. Too much cinnamon. It's causing heartburn."

"Anyone else think so?"

Jack frowned. "Well come to think of it, I'm the only one complaining."

Charlie scratched at his chin. "Probably that acid reflux stuff."

Jack nodded then bent over and opened his desk drawer. "Right now I need some antacid and truth on how much cinnamon they're putting in that."

Jack pulled out a bottle of pills.

Charlie watched his friend open the lid and pour two into his hand. Jack held them up as if to toast Charlie. "Cheers."

"I'll take your word for it. But what I want right now is some truth."

The corner of Jack's mouth lifted on one side. He nodded. "Go on."

"Do you know anything about anyone wanting the shelter?"

"Josiah's shelter?"

"Does Whiskey have another?"

"I do." Jack pulled the glass to his lips and took a smaller sip. He closed his eyes.

Charlie waited. Not as patient as he'd like to have, but he did manage to keep himself from hurling the pitchfork at his phone. But in all reality, he knew that wouldn't speed Jack up. Nope not that old buzzard. He like to take his sweet time. So Charlie waited.

Finally, after another minute or so of Jack rolling the ice around in the glass, Jack focused in on Charlie with a grimace. "There's two groups who want the shelter."

Charlie pushed off the pitchfork. He tipped his hat back. "Two groups, huh?"

Jack rubbed at the center of his chest. "But, only one of them is serious about wanting it."

Charlie massaged his jaw. "Serious, huh? Which one"

"Dymblebee."

Charlie's brows shot up. "You're kidding, right?"

Jack's eyes twinkled. "Yes, Sir, as serious as a heart attack."

"What in the world?"

Jack sat back in his chair. "You hear about Whiskey's revitalization?"

The word revitalization bounced around in Charlie's thoughts, but never stuck to anything that Susan or Evie might have said. Didn't even ring a bell as to anything he might have heard on his own. But then again, Whiskey never made it to the top of any list of his and why would it? His brother-in-law had died seven years ago in a plane crash over the Bermuda triangle and Susan rarely ever talked about Josiah or the shelter. In fact, the subject had been off limits since the day Josiah disappeared. And the only other person Charlie knew from Whiskey hadn't ever mentioned anything important like this to him.

Charlie glanced at the stall floor. His hand tightened around the pitchfork. He turned back to the phone. "Anyone else?"

Jack looked down at his glass then scooted it from his reach.

Charlie watched him stare at his glass.

Finally, Jack turned to him with eyes smiling. "Me."

Like a cowboy shooting out of the gate on the prize bull, frustration exploded in Charlie's back. He held up his pitchfork, tines pointing at the screen. "You? Seriously? Why? What for?"

Jack chuckled. "I thought it would make a good spot for a steakhouse and bar."

Charlie's eyes narrowed to the screen. "And what about the Stockyard?"

Jack waved a hand. "Now hold on. Don't throw a shoe. I planned on talking to you about this way before Evie ever got involved."

"But?"

But I've had my own problems.

Charlie lowered the pitchfork.

Not much ticked him off, but lately, anything that had to do with that shelter seemed to hit the top of his list in regards to his temper. But in all reality, Jack and he were best friends. So maybe he had a good reason for this. He thought maybe, just maybe he should hear him out.

The slide of Jack's desk drawer opening pulled Charlie from his thoughts, he watched as a somewhat paler Jack drop the bottle of antacids into it. His friend slammed the drawer closed. Surprised that the drawer didn't bounce back, Charlie sucked in his breath.

Jack glanced at the screen. "I mentioned to you the trouble with Griff didn't I?"

Charlie slowly let the breath out he held while he racked his memory. Then the words of his best friend came through clear as a bell "Jillian's fading and Griff's not handling it."

Charlie tipped back his hat. "Guess we're all preoccupied by things out of our control right now."

Jack wiped at his brow. Never truer words spoken."

"Is there anything I can do to help out?"

Jack looked down, then lifted his head. With wetness, his eyes twinkled. "No. Nothing anyone can do now."

Charlie shuffled his feet. His neck muscles tightened. "Let me know if —"

Jack shook his head and sank back into his chair "No worries. I've got this one taken care of." His voice lowered. "Probably the only thing a brother could do anyway."

On those words, the image of Susan and Josiah popped into his head. He chewed on the inside of his cheek and switched hands with the pitchfork. "Yeah, that's for sure."

Jack's head turned.

A fly buzzed around Charlie's head. He swatted at the bug with a few choice words. When he glanced back at the video call, Jack had moved in closer with a grin on his face.

"Been working out here for the last few hours and now the bugs want to be known."

Jack laughed. "But aren't you the top shi—"

Charlie held up a hand. "Don't say it or I'll make sure you've got plenty."

Jack continued laughing. "Nice to know I'm not the only one dealing with manure these days."

Charlie rolled his eyes then grabbed his hat. He swung the thing over his head. Finally, it disappeared. He let his shoulders drop as he blew out his breath. "And I thought once I left the Army, I figured I'd have to look into some kind of exercise program."

Jack rolled his eyes. "Seriously? You thought that knowing you'd spend the rest of your days on that ranch of yours?"

A crooked smile appeared on Charlie's lips. "Believe it or not, I did. Not hard for us old timers to forget the stuff of our past."

Jack nodded. "Same with me, but instead of finding me dead in a pile of cow dung, they'll find me in-between barrels of whiskey."

"I'd rather have that too." Charlie stuffed his hat back on top of his head. "But seriously, I do need your opinion. It's important."

Jack sat up. "Okay, how can I help?"

Not thrilled to have this particular conversation now out here in the barn where anyone could hear it, Charlie moved closer to the phone. He rubbed his jaw. "I told you the clown's coming up for parole, right?"

Jack nodded. "You did."

"Well with all these crazy people letting out criminals these days and not making them serve at least their minimum, I need to find someone who can make sure that doesn't happen with this clown."

The slightest hint of a curl upward of Jack's mouth indicated to Charlie that his friend knew someone. "You know anyone I could talk to about this?"

Jack nodded. "I might."

Charlie rubbed at the back of his neck. "Want to give me a clue on who?"

Jack shook his head. "Tell you what, let me talk to them and if they can help, I'll have them call you."

Charlie stared at the screen. The proposal Jack offered ran through his head. Not revealing the person's identity to Charlie meant Jack had possibly a high-ranking official in mind. But Charlie wouldn't put it past Jack to stall either until he found someone if he didn't already have someone in mind. He hated disappointing his friends, so he might put them out on a hook, but eventually he'd slowly pull you in. And Jack knew what that clown did to Evie all those years ago and as if she were his daughter, Charlie knew he'd do everything to protect her also.

"Use my cell number. I don't want Susan in on this. She's got too much on her plate as is."

Jack nodded. "Sounds like a plan."

"You think they can help me out right quick? Clown's parole hearing is coming up."

Jack's eyes danced. "Yes. And don't you worry. We won't let anything happen to our girl."

Charlie smiled wide. "Appreciate that."

Jack picked up his rocks glass again. He swirled the contents, leaned in and sniffed it again, then set it back down. "Did you know Griff's taking an interest in your girl? So if that rotten clown manages to get paroled he won't have the chance to get close enough to her."

Charlie rocked back on his heels. His eyes blew open. "Griff your Griff?"

Jack dropped his pen. "Yes. He's on the revitalization committee for Whiskey. The mayor sent him to check on things at the shelter. They met and sounds like they hit it off."

"Hmm? Now that's interesting."

Text Message
April 29th
6:15 PM

Charlie: Darlin', meet me for drinks.

Susan: No. Still working on this campaign.

Charlie: Still?

Susan: Did I stutter?

Charlie: Don't get mad at me. Didn't you change the campaign?

Susan: And your point?

Charlie: Don't you think you were being a little drastic?

Susan: No.

Charlie: Rolling eyes here.

Susan: Grow up.

Charlie: Stop complaining then and meet me for drinks.

Susan: But Charles. I need to get this done. Unless of course you can convince Evie to come back???

Charlie: The Cattlemen's Association is having a benefit square dance next month to help raise money for the homeless veterans.

Susan: And?

Charlie: I reckoned we could go.

Susan: You do? And how do you suppose that will happen when I need to get this campaign done so it will launch in time without the help of Evie?

Charlie: So, I'm guessing that's a no?

Susan: It's wonderful that I married a man with such intelligence.

Charlie: You my Darlin', are a lucky lady!

Susan: Charles. Let's get serious. I don't have time. I wish I did. Anyway, one of the heels broke on my favorite boots. I have no time to get them repaired or find new ones. We'll go next time.
            Promise.

Charlie: Do you still wear a size 7 narrow?

Susan: Are you listening to me?

Charlie: Black boots would look great especially with black jeans.

Susan: Charles! Stop. Listen to me, will you?

Charlie: Did you know Evie's seeing someone?

Susan: What? Who?

Charlie: Evie.

Susan: Yes. I understand that. Who is she seeing?

Charlie: Jack's nephew.

Susan: What? Jack's nephew? We need to get her back here soon.

Charlie: Not going to happen.

Susan: Call Humphrey and have drinks with him then.

Charlie: Don't wait up. Might be late.

Susan: Drive carefully. And bring Evie home.

Charlie: Anyone ever tell you are impossible?

Susan: Love you too.

Charlie: Hmm? Sometimes I wonder.

Susan: Oh now Charles, don't get dramatic.

Charlie: Wonder if Humphrey wears a size 7 narrow?

Chapter 8 Whiskey Trust

"HELLO HUMPHRY." Charlie stood up from his chair. "How are you doing you old dog?" He leaned over his desk and extended a hand toward him.

Humphrey an older gentleman dressed in a gray suit, white shirt, with a red tie grabbed Charlie 's hand. "I'm doing well. I do apologize for not getting your message last night about drinks."

Charlie shook his head. "No problem. I shouldn't have called at the last minute."

"You mentioned trying some of Barleyshots newest whiskey, did you like it? Is it true Jack's making a cinnamon whiskey for the holidays?"

The two broke their grip.

Not wanting to divulge any secrets Jack had brewing at the distillery, he just shot Humphrey a lopsided smile. "Your guess is as good as mine. But reckon he might not have enough time to put it out this Christmas."

Humphrey chuckled. "Good to know."

Charlie pointed to the seats in front of his desk. "Hopefully this meeting today didn't mess with your schedule."

"No. Not at all, just getting ready for a trip to Washington."

"Washington?" Charlie 's eyebrows rose. "The capital or state?"

The other man set his briefcase down and took a seat in one of the leather wingback chairs. "State. Going this weekend to check on a little apple orchard my daughter decided she wants."

Charlie chuckled shaking his head. "These girls. What's gotten into them these days?"

Humphrey's head tilted. "Charlie? Something wrong with Evie?"

Charlie stood. "What can I get you to drink? Whiskey? Coffee?"

Humphrey waved off Charlie. "No. Nothing for me."

Charlie picked up the phone receiver. "Not even a coffee? It won't take Lucia long to make a pot."

Humphrey pointed to his lap. "No. The doctor says it's not good for the prostate. In fact, I've got to cut out all caffeinated beverages. And it's too early for a whiskey."

Charlie dropped the receiver back into the cradle, then ran his hand over his face. "It's a bitch getting old."

Humphry nodded.

Charlie picked up a picture of Evie in a silver frame. She smiled out at him. Then he looked down again and studied Susan's image staring at him from a gold frame. He let out a deep sigh.

He said nothing at first. Words crashed in his thoughts on just how he'd present this to his friend.

"Charlie? What's wrong?"

Finally, he just blurted it out. "Susan wants me to freeze Evie's trust account."

Humphry gulped, then unbuttoned the top button of his dress shirt, slid a finger under his collar and tie and pulled on it. "She does?"

Charlie nodded.

"Are you sure?"

"Yes, I'm sure. How long will it take?"

Humphrey sat up straighter in his chair. "Well," he rubbed the back of his neck. "I've not had to file for a trust suspension in a very long time, in the old days it would take at least a month. It might be quicker, maybe before the weeks up." He pointed to his computer bag. "With everything online now, it will be a lot faster to file. But it will depend on my finding the appropriate forms to do so."

"Okay." Charlie put the silver frame down then massaged the back of his neck. Finally, he blew out his breath. "I hope it's faster than trying to buy boots on the internet."

Humphrey chuckled. "Depends on what kind of boots your shopping for."

"Women's."

One of Humphrey's eyebrows rose. "Oh heavens. Definitely yes."

A knot started to tighten around Charlie's heart. His mouth grew dry. He scanned his desk. Nothing to drink. And boy could he really use one. He licked his lips and mentally shoved the words past his teeth. "Let's get it started."

Humphrey nodded, reached forward and pulled his briefcase onto his lap. "Most of its all done electronically now. I can ask for an emergency suspension. The process could start today, if you'd like."

Charlie nodded. A sadness washed over him. His brown eyes struggled to hold open his heavy lids. "That's fine."

Humphrey pulled out his laptop placing it on his thighs. He set his case on the floor next to him. Then he leaned onto the unopened computer. "It's not like you Charlie. What's Evie done?"

Charlie pinched the bridge of his nose as he stared at his old friend.

"Is it drugs?"

Charlie shook his head.

"Don't tell me she's giving it away to those despicable DemoRats?"

Charlie chuckled. A faint grin appeared. "No nothing that drastic."

"Then what?"

"Honestly, I didn't want to call you. But Susan insisted."

"Susan?"

"Yes." He nodded. "She's upset Evie resigned from Mae's and took off for Whiskey to open up Josiah's shelter."

Humphrey's mouth dropped. He stuck a finger in his ear, twisted it around, then he pulled it out. "Did I hear you correctly?"

Charlie grimaced. "You sure did."

A smile flashed across Humphry's face. "Well good for her."

"I know." Charlie picked up a letter opener. He used the pointed end to clear some dirt out from under a fingernail. "I'm proud of her striking out on her own. She needs to build up her backbone, I just wish she'd not rushed into all this."

"Rushed?"

"Susan and I think she might have jumped into a frying pan feet first. And maybe she doesn't know what she's gotten into."

Humphrey shook his head slowly. "No, sir I'd disagree."

Charlie halted picking at his fingernail. He looked right at his friend. "Awe Humphrey, you and I both know Evie's been handed everything to her. She hasn't had to work for anything."

"Now excuse me for saying so, but that girl of yours is a hard worker."

The corners of Charlie's mouth started to twitch.

Humphrey leaned forward. "That's what you and I both know. She's got so much confidence and determination I don't see how she could ever fail."

"What do you mean?"

"I believe Ms. Evie's been hoping for something like this for at least six months."

"Six months?"

"Yes, that's right. She approached me this past fall about using her trust as collateral for a loan."

One of Charlie's eyebrows arched. "She did?"

"She sure did, but I told her we only needed to secure the loan with a portion of the trust, not all of it. You know just for the amount she wanted."

"Hmm?" Charlie rubbed the back of his neck. His lips started to curl slightly.

He never doubted Evie's intelligence and maybe freezing her trust wouldn't be a true hardship, but maybe hard enough to bring her back home. After all, that's what her mamma wanted. No actually demanded. Charlie frowned. Atypical as shelter work might be for a Stockton, deep inside Charlie understood one couldn't deny its merits.

His cell phone buzzed. He picked it up. A text flashed across the screen from his wife.

SUSAN: Have you talked to Humphrey yet? Do I need to call him?

A vein in Charlie 's jaw twitched as he clenched his teeth. Heat started to crawl up his neck. His chest rose as he breathed in long and hard. Then blowing the air out through his nose, he set the phone down. Charlie looked at his old friend and pointed to his laptop. "Prepare the suspension for now, but don't submit it until I give the word."

Humphrey chuckled. "And Susan?"

Charlie's lips hooked to one side. "Don't worry, I'll deal with the aftermath."

Humphrey nodded. "I'll file a draft under inappropriate fund distribution. You just send word when you want it to go live."

Text Message
May 2
9:11 PM

Charlie:	Darlin', I'll be late tonight.
Susan:	Again? Where are you?
Charlie:	On my way to Bill's.
Susan:	For what?
Charlie:	To discuss the beef prices.
Susan:	I thought you finished all that during the convention.
Charlie:	We did, but Hank found a problem and we are meeting now to iron it out.
Susan:	Please tell me you talked to Humphrey.
Charlie:	I did.
Susan:	When will Evie be home?
Charlie:	Don't count on her coming home.
Susan:	What? Why not?
Charlie:	He says, she's been looking to leave for some time now.
Susan:	Did you fire him?
Charlie:	Now why would I do such a thing?
Susan:	He should have told us about this sooner.
Charlie:	Nothing more came up regarding it, so he thought she changed her mind.
Susan:	She's stubborn. She won't change unless forced to.
Charlie:	Hmm?
Susan:	What's that supposed to mean?
Charlie:	Sounds like her Mamma.
Susan:	And what about the clown? How do we handle that?
Charlie:	As long as I'm alive, he'll never come near her again.
Susan:	Well, bless your heart. I'm relieved now.
Charlie:	Susan. Quit getting dramatic on me.
Susan:	She needs to be brought home.
Charlie:	Do you really want to do that?
Susan:	Is Humphrey going to help out or not?
Charlie:	I'm just pulling into Bill's. We'll talk later.

Susan: Charles.

Charlie: Love you, Darlin'. Don't wait up tonight.

Susan: Charles, don't you want the best for our daughter?

Charlie: Yes, Darlin' I do. Now will discuss it when I get home.

Susan: Fine.

Charlie: Fine, we'll discuss it? Or fine you'll handle it?

Charlie: Susan?

Susan: Fine. Will discuss later. Now go fix your beef prices.

Charlie: Okay, Darlin', love you.

Susan: XOXOXOX

Chapter 9 Whiskey Stubborn

CHARLIE TOOK IN A DEEP BREATH. The faintest hint of a dark roasted Columbian coffee tickled his nose. He let out a sigh. "Coffee. Now that's a real man's giddy up."

He stepped out of the mudroom. A deep shiver ran down his spine. "Crap. Rotten spring storms. He looked down at his boots. The mud covered them from toes to his shins. He shook his head and kept walking. He only thought of one thing at the moment.

Coffee. Hot coffee.

The fixation on a cup of coffee almost overwhelmed Charlie's curiosity. But the mess he came upon with the marble-topped bank secretary that lined the wall overtook the curiosity for the coffee — at least for the moment.

Charlie stopped. He stared down at the small table and floor. He cocked his head. The secretary usually sat against the wall with keys thrown into a small basket with the day's mail, but today it looked as if the mail had exploded atop the antique.

Charlie glanced down the hall. No one but himself stood there. He rubbed the back of his neck

"What in the tarnation?"

Intuition told him he needed to clean up the mess. He bent with his back and knees silently groaning with the strain to pick up the sprinkled debris of mail. One-by-one, he stacked them in his hand and one-by-one he fingered through each one. He studied who each belonged to. He shook his head. And after gathering the last letter, one eyebrow shot up. In typical fashion, a name and address appeared on the front. The same name and address on each one. He mumbled his daughter's name under his breath. The muscles in his neck tightened. *He shook his head hoping to loosen the tightness. But without any immediate relief, he* neatly stacked them on top of the secretary. After about a minute of thought, he recognized the problem.

Susan.

A sense of frustration weaved around his heart. He closed his eyes as his hand slipped around to the back of his neck. His muscles grew tighter the more he rubbed. He rolled his shoulders hoping to encourage them to loosen up, but they refused. He blew out his breath.

Need some aspirin.

The thoughts of the hot cup of coffee he wanted only moments ago faded to the back of his head. Now only thoughts of worry entertained the vacated spot. Thoughts of Evie and how she wanted out on her own. Out to ruin her own life. Out under the control of a mama who masked her fierce protective love with that same type of control. The thoughts of what to do about Susan and Evie warred with one another. In one sense, he wanted Evie to break out on her own, but in another, he like Evie's mama had become somewhat overly protective of their daughter since the incident of her eighth birthday.

"How in the world am I going to resolve this?"

Sure, he understood fathers worried about their children, which came no different for him, but with Evie moving out, they appeared more often than not. Heck they sometimes appeared out of the blue. Like now.

For the most part, Charlie had the typical worries for his child, but now with her sudden departure, the level of worry rose tenfold.

Evie moved out almost a month ago. Her mamma wanted him to cut off her funds. And at this point, it didn't look as if she'd return any time soon. Or if at all.

Crazy Mae stubbornness. But toughness, that's a different story.

He rubbed at his jaw. He knew his daughter. Although she had the Stockton blood and the Stockton's traditionally had enough toughness to go around, did she have it? After all these years, he and Susan had coddled her quite a bit. He hadn't planned on that and in fact, he never intended to, but if it hadn't been for that rotten clown who ruined everything twenty years ago who now looked to be doing the same thing all over again, but this time in the way of an early release from prison.

He grimaced with the thought of the upcoming parole hearing he would need to do something about.

He growled as he brushed some water droplets from his jeans. "Stupid birthday party."

Upon entering the kitchen, Charlie squinted at the new colors. First with the oranges, red, and yellows hitting him. Only the milk chocolate woodwork muted the brightness. When his eyes finally adjusted to the brightness, which had been occurring on a daily basis, he shook his head. "Still not exactly what I would have picked."

As he scanned the room, he took in a deep breath. Only a faint hint of the paint fumes tickled his nose, but the smell of a dark roast coffee became even more prevalent as he walked further into the kitchen.

Charlie smiled to himself and with no one else in the room, he danced a quick two-step over to some highly polished dark oak cabinets. He grabbed a door and pulled on it. With a sigh, he grabbed for a large brown mug. As he turned toward the coffee pot, he scanned the room — No one. "Good, a cup of coffee to myself."

He stepped up to the old electric percolator and with steady hands, he lifted the pot and began to pour. A deep frown surfaced. He set the mug down then shook the Percolator and swore. He released the pot. It crashed onto the countertop. "Well Now who leaves only a spits worth in the pot? That's like leaving a swallow's worth of milk in the carton."

Just then, Susan strolled into the kitchen with Lucia in tow.

"But *Señora* you talked to *Señor* Collins?"

Charlie set down the coffee pot and turned towards the women.

Susan halted with a start. Her surprise melted into a frown. She grasped the housekeeper's arm. "Shh. Not now Lucia."

Charlie watched the two without saying anything.

Lucia took a step back as if Susan had surprised her, but then Charlie caught the slightest wink from her to him and he decided not to say anything just yet.

Lucia leaned into Susan with a stage whisper, "but *Señora* won't *Señor* Collins help?"

Charlie smiled to himself as he leaned against the counter and crossed his legs.

Hmm? What's this old girl up to? She's talking to Collins?

Susan lifted her mug to a plastered smile. "Hello Darling, Lucia made some fine coffee. You should have some."

"Charlie nodded toward the pot and mumbled, "I'd love some." Then his eyebrows scrunched as he pointed to her. "I thought you weren't drinking coffee anymore?"

Susan cocked her head at Charlie. "Whatever gave you that thought?"

Charlie closed his eyes and sighed" "I don't know Darlin', maybe you telling me so."

Susan crossed to the sink, placed her cup next to it. "I'm sure you heard me wrong."

"Hmm?" Charlie huffed. "There's a lot I seem to be hearing wrong these days."

One skeptical eyebrow rose over Susan's face. "Charlie?"

A low growl came from Charlie. "Never mind."

Susan turned toward the window. "Have you heard anything from Evie?"

"No Nothing."

"Not even a text message?"

At those words, Charlie's neck muscles tightened. He didn't want to lie, but at the moment, Susan had something up her sleeve and until he knew more, he didn't feel like sharing. So he did what the main street news did, he faked it. But first, he glanced upward.

Lord, I promise I'll divulge everything to her once I get the whole picture... I think.

"No, no messages either."

Susan twisted back toward Charlie. "And Humphrey? Did she reach out to him for help again?"

Charlie took in a breath, blew it out, picked up his empty coffee mug and peered in it.

"Charles?"

"No. I don't believe so. Humphry's in Washington until next week."

"Hmm?" Susan tapped a fingernail on her cup. "She can't get any funds, correct?"

"That's correct, Darlin'. She's pretty much broke, unless she took out some before all this or she's got someone helping her that we don't know about."

Just then, Lucia whispered, "*Señorita* Evie is completely broke, *sí?*"

Charlie leaned on the counter. "Nothing to worry about Lucia. She's fine."

Leaves and debris whipped around outside the windows.

Lucia moved to the counter and shuffled a fruit bowl back and forth. She looked over at Charlie. "She will come home soon, *sí?*"

Charlie didn't want to lie, and being a Colonel in the Army, lying would get you court martialed. But at the moment, so he wouldn't have to deal with two irate women, he did.

Charlie nodded. "I'm sure of it."

"But not before the holiday?"

Charlie shook his head. "Not sure about that Lucia. But she's safe. I'll make sure of that."

Lucia's head bobbed. "You are a good *papá*. And she is headstrong. Maybe it is good for her to spread her wings, *sí?*"

Charlie's brain struggled with his heart. It ached at the thought of Evie out on her own. But at twenty-eight, most women were. And lots started their own families by this time. So, Evie at the shelter, which only took a short ride there, really did not differentiate from any other young lady.

But how many of these ladies had clowns to deal with and an overly protective mamma?

Yeah sure, an overly protective mamma might be common for a lot of them, especially with the drugs coming through Texas and the human trafficking going on, but the clowns? Now he could almost guarantee one-hundred percent that never happened.

With these thoughts stirring in his head, worry lines creased the corners of his eyes as he nodded. "We do too."

Susan glanced down at her coffee cup, turned on the faucet, and let the steady stream of water wash over it. After inspecting it, she placed it into the dish rack. "Is anyone helping her?"

Charlie chuckled to himself.

Not yet.

Susan stepped closer to him. "Charles? Is anyone helping her?"

Charlie's gaze narrowed in on his wife. "I have no clue. She's been there now for a bit. And let's not forget, about the possible trouble with her funds you've been inquiring into ."

Susan halted. The grin she wore contained no mirth. "Now dear, do you think I'd really do something harmful just to get my daughter home where she belongs?"

A loud clap of thunder shook the house.

She jumped.

Charlie caught her and pulled her into his arms. Her body melted into his.

His breath froze in his chest.

Energy sizzled between them as she drug one manicured finger up his arm. Each nerve ending in his arm danced at her touch.

The temperature around them rose.

Susan drug that same finger across his jaw line.

Charlie leaned into her touch, his brown eyes danced.

Rain pelted the windows.

She cradled one side of his jaw into the palm of her hand. "Now Charlie. That's our daughter. I only want the best for her. Do you really think I'd do anything to hurt her?"

On hearing those words, subconsciously red flags flew up everywhere. His brain pushed the red alert button.

Holder now. She's trying to distract you.

His heart thumped in agreement.

Okay, two can play.

He slid one arm around her waist and caught her hand with his other one. He pulled her hard against his chest.

Susan gasped.

Charlie pulled her fingers to his lips and gently kissed each one.

Susan closed her eyes as her head fell back leaving her neck open.

Charlie pressed a tender kiss on her creamy white skin leaving a slight whisker burn to just below her ear.

Susan moaned. "Charlie. That's not fair."

He smiled and leaned into her. His hold around her waist became possessive. And with only a whisper between them he took in a deep sniff of the expensive perfume she wore. The scent intoxicated him. His heart kicked with a reminder from his brain and he whispered, "For some odd reason, I think you're capable of doing much worse."

Charlie:	How you holding up?
Evie:	Well, that depends.
Charlie:	Really? On what?
Evie:	Are we talking about the staff I need or the clowns?
Charlie:	Clowns? What clowns?
Evie:	A troupe of clowns who belong to a traveling circus need a place to stay while their fifth wheel is in for repairs.
Charlie:	Hmm? Thought I heard something about that.
Evie:	Unfortunately, whatever you heard is probably true.
Charlie:	Any trouble out of them?
Evie:	No Daddy. They're fine, but…
Charlie:	But what?
Evie:	It's nothing.
Charlie:	Don't go cryptic. What's the problem with the clowns?
Evie:	They don't like my cooking.
Evie:	Daddy?
Charlie:	Hold on. I'm speechless.
Evie:	That's not funny.
Charlie:	Do you have your insurance paid up?
Charlie:	Evie?
Evie:	Good question. Another thing to put on my list.
Charlie:	Good God girl. What are you thinking?
Evie:	I'm thinking I need a cook and an office assistant.
Charlie:	Can you afford them?
Evie:	I believe so. But another reason to get an assistant. Josiah's office is a horrible mess.
Charlie:	Want me to send your Mamma to help?
Evie:	Daddy. That's not funny.
Charlie:	Sorry. Just wanted to lighten the mood.
Evie:	Thanks.
Charlie:	You'll let me know if you need anything, right?

Evie: Thanks, Daddy, but I got this.

Charlie: Anyone ever tell you that you remind them of your Mamma? Stubborn… to the core.

Evie: Oh, thanks.

Charlie: It's the truth.

Evie: No. And FYI, you're the only one that says that.

Charlie: Getting a phone call. Let me know if you need help.

Evie: Can I hire Lucia?

Charlie: NO!!!

Evie: Fine.

Charlie: Here's two tips of advice. 1 – Advertise for help.

Evie: And number two?

Charlie: Don't go near that stove. Eat out until you hire a cook.

Evie: Daddy! You're not funny.

Charlie: Good. Not a joke.

Evie: Fine. But if these clowns revolt, I blame you.

Charlie: Bonus tip…Get insured before you do anything else.

Evie: Argh!

Charlie: You know your birthday is coming up real quick.

Evie: Yes. How about Lucia for my present?

Charlie: Sure. If you come home.

Evie: Daddy.

Charlie: Just checking.

Evie: You and Mother going to make it for my birthday?

Charlie: Sorry Sweetheart. Need to go to Oklahoma to see about a bull.

Evie: And Mother?

Charlie: Don't count on it unless you're moving home.

Evie: Bummer.

Charlie: Love you!

Evie: Me, too. Chat soon… or later.

Chapter 10 Whiskey Vending

CHARLIE HUFFED.
That old rotten buzzard. Going and having a heart attack.
He rubbed his forehead.
What's he thinking?
In the Whiskey Hospital's intensive care unit waiting room, Charlie pulled his worn cowboy hat off and slapped it against his thigh.

If, Jack thinks he's going to get out of this friendship… and our deal, he's dead wrong.

Charlie paced the floor. He stopped to watch the news from the TV in the corner. The weatherman broadcasted more rain to come. He shook his head. "Home for less than a year and it's done nothing but rain off and on. "Miserable rain. We've had enough. What is it monsoon season?"

Before he pulled out his cell phone, he stuffed his hat back on top of his head. Not the most graceful placement. But at the moment, he didn't care. The stress of possibly losing a friend, his best friend, weighed heavy on his heart, as did most things did right now.

When he pulled out his cell phone, it lit up with the first tap. He tapped a second time. The message app opened. His finger hovered only a second over the new message button. But Charlie knew with Jack in the hospital, his need for extra help now became apparent. He typed in the name Spence.

Hopefully he can get me some answers.

For a guy who worked with his hands most of these days, Charlie's finger dexterity hadn't slowed much, unless of course he had to type on one of these screens. The vice-like clench of his jaw made it ache. He rolled his shoulders as he held onto his phone. Finally, after tapping and tapping to create a message he hoped the recipient would not ignore. He gave it a quick once over, nodded, then stabbed the send button. His head throbbed. Not having any aspirin on him and doubtful the hospital would give him anything for it, unless of course he checked himself into the Emergency Room. He groaned. Instead, he turned. "I need some coffee. That'll get rid of this headache."

But after scanning the room, he found only water and fruit. He walked out to the nurse's station. A twig of a nurse in pink scrubs stood looking at a chart. "Howdy ma'am,"

The skinny thing cocked her head.

"Is Jack Barleyshot in his room yet?"

The nurse who looked not quite ready to be out of puberty smiled. "No Sir, not yet. He'll be coming up from the Cath lab soon."

"Okay." Charlie tipped back his Old Stetson. "I'll be back."

"It shouldn't be more than a half hour or so."

The nurse nodded. "I'll tell him to expect you if he gets back first."

Charlie tapped the brim of his hat. "Thank you ma'am."

The young thing giggled as she returned to perusing the chart.

Charlie turned and headed down the hall. He stopped half way down after he noticed a familiar hum of vending machines. The noise drew him into a small alcove. He smiled.

When he saw the machine that offered all types of cold drinks, his eyes lit up. He stepped up to the machine and scanned the selection of drinks. He licked his lips as he read each one carefully. Not expecting to see coffee from the machine, his heart did a little dance when he found the second to last button boasting an iced coffee drink. He smiled to himself.

Better than nothing.

"Coffee. Thanks be to the almighty."

Charlie dug into his jeans and pulled out a few dollar bills. He Looked at his watch and grinned.

Plenty time for one, maybe two.

One hand hovered over the selection of his choice while the other fed a dollar into the machine.

The vending machine slowly pulled the dollar into its slot. Once it disappeared, he pushed on the button for the iced coffee.

He licked his lips again while he waited. Nothing happened. A frown invaded his happiness. He pushed harder on the button. He waited again. Again, nothing happened. This time, he punched the button with his fist. The machine jiggled but still no coffee came out.

Charlie pointed at the machine. "Now look here I don't cotton to this."

He pushed another dollar in. It took it. And still nothing. No grinding of gears. No can fell into the slot. Nothing.

He groaned as he thunked his head on the vending machine. An image of him lying in a bed with a bandage wrapped around his head provoked him to stop. With his eyes closed, he asked for assistance.

"Lord, I could really use a cup of coffee, but most important, make sure that old buzzard recuperates from this heart trouble. Amen."

Charlie opened his eyes. An index card-sized note lay on the floor in front of his boots. Actually, the thing stuck to the sole when he tried to kick at it. He bent and ripped it away. His head started to pound harder when he read it.

Out of order.

Charlie grumbled. "Why me? Why can't I get a coffee?" He closed his eyes as he leaned his forehead against the humming vending machine. "Can't even get a can of that good for nothing iced stuff. Is there a conspiracy?"

A plump nurse in purple scrubs rounded the corner and stopped. "Sir, you okay?"

Charlie twisted his head, looked at the woman sideways. "Is there any regular coffee around here?"

She laughed, "Not on this floor. We don't want to tempt our cardiac patients."

"But what about the non-patients?"

The nurse stepped into the small alcove. "Now that's funny."

Charlie looked down and blew out his breath. "Is there any nearby?"

"Hmm," the nurse chuckled tapping on her clipboard. "I'm not sure. Maybe down in the sleep lab." She stepped closer. "Aren't you here to see Mr. Barleyshot?"

Charlie stood up straight, brushed at his hat. "Yes Ma'am, I am. Is he back from his procedure?"

She nodded. "Yes sir he is. You can visit for a few minutes but he'll be tired. So don't wear him out."

Charlie nodded. "Thank you Ma'am."

"And just to caution you, Mr. Barleyshot's wife said she'd be back soon, and she warned if anyone gave him anything other than what the doctor's ordered, she'd personally skin them alive."

Charlie laughed, "Got to love a good woman."

"Good, yes. And a woman who loves her man."

Charlie arched a brow. "You know her personally?"

The nurse laughed. "No, but you can just tell by the way she fusses over him."

Charlie smiled to himself. The image reminded him of how Susan fussed over him in their earlier years of marriage. But now, she had little time to do that with all the work she put in at the Foundation and help with running the ranch. He frowned on that thought. Why had he put her through all that. The thoughts now blazing a trail through his head rivaled the last time he and his boys shuffled the long horns from one pasture to another so as to let that field rejuvenate. Sure, the herd hated it, but once moved, they had no qualms with the fresh blades of grass. The corner of his lips curled up. Susan would hate the idea, but this time he wouldn't let her turn it down.

A familiar image slowly meandered into his thoughts — the Bell, white sandy beach, blue water, and Susan.

Okay. Let's get this clown thing figured out. Then we're heading for the sunset... Even if I have to hog-tie her.

Charlie's phone buzzed, He held up his hand. "Beg your pardon I need to see about this."

The nurse patted his forearm. "No problem Sir," then she leaned in and whispered, "Beans and Leaves is a great place for a cup of coffee and a pastry if you can't find any around here."

Charlie winked with a nod.

Spencer Investigations name flashed onto his screen.

The tightness in his head started to fade.

He tapped on the message button, turned, and strode out of the room.

Spencer PI: Howdy Charlie. Heard you were looking for me.
Charlie: Sure am. You free?
Spencer PI: Depends on when you need me.
Charlie: How about now?
Spencer PI: I think that could be worked out.
Charlie: Regular fee?
Spencer PI: How soon do you need info?
Charlie: Yesterday.
Spencer PI: Nothing like rushing anyone.
Charlie: Okay, how about tomorrow?
Spencer PI: Seriously? It'll cost double.
Charlie: How about as soon as possible then?
Spencer PI: Still same price.
Charlie: Fine.
Spencer PI: What are you looking for?
Charlie: Need details on the clown.
Spencer PI: Same clown I'm thinking of?
Charlie: Yes. No other.
Spencer PI: No other? Is there more than one now?
Charlie: There's always more than one.
Spencer PI: Little confused. Are we talking about the same clown?
Charlie: How about everyone's favorite state pen clown?
Spencer PI: Everyone's favorite?
Charlie: Okay, maybe those who might need some target practice.
Spencer PI: Now you're talking. What do you need.
Charlie: Everything. Plus, who wants him out now.
Spencer PI: Parole, already?
Charlie: Not by my doings.
Spencer PI: Holy smokes.
Charlie: You in?

Spencer PI: Yes, sir.
Charlie: Call me direct when you get anything.
Spencer PI: No wife involvement?
Charlie: Not this time.
Spencer PI: Roger. No wife involvement.
Charlie: Thanks.
Spencer PI: Don't thank me yet. You haven't seen my bill yet.
Charlie: Barleyshot whiskey bonus if you deliver by week's end.
Spencer PI: Deal.
Charlie: Remember, info for my eyes only.

Chapter 11 Whiskey Heart

THE STRONG ODOR OF DISINFECTANT SATURATED THE AIR. Hospital white colored all objects except for a large bouquet of yellow roses that stood tall in a glass vase that looked an awful lot like a cowboy boot on the table next to the bed. Their sweet perfume drifted toward Charlie as he entered the room. Not willing to share space with the flowers, Charlie moved to the other side of the bed where his best friend lay.

Jack Barleyshot's eyes remained closed.

Charlie carefully examined the situation. No movement came from Jack. In fact, no movement came from him at all. No movement and no sound except for the soft puffs the oxygen made from the mask that covered the whiskey magnate's face.

Electronic beeps attempted to stay in sync with the oxygen.

Charlie turned to study the back wall behind the bed. Up top, a display of lights and numbers ticked up and down. Back and forth, his eyes danced at each one. Not seeing any pattern on the numbers falling or rising at a rapid rate, but instead they stayed constant. He let out a slow breath.

"That's right keep it steady."

A metallic creak broke Charlie's concentration. He shifted back to his best friend. Still no movement or sound came from the man. In fact, the man lay so tightly swaddled in the crisp white sheet and body- knit blanket he could not be too sure if the noise he just heard actually came from Jack's bed or out in the hall. Charlie shot a look at the door. Nurses walked briskly from room-to-room carrying clipboards and small computers, while a small group in white coats and stethoscopes stood in front of the door cattycorner from Jack's.

A few rapid squawks of requests rang out periodically from the public announce system.

The tightness in Charlie's neck grew. No tingles, just tightness. A good sign.

As Charlie inched closer to Jack, he rested his forearms on the cool rails of the bed. He closed his eyes then clasped his hands with two-pointed fingers that steepled the air in front of him. Not a disbeliever of prayer, but the opposite, Charlie bowed his head.

Lord, we ask for healing of our friend, Jack. We still need him here. And we know he loves you, so it's with great love I ask for this blessing for him, and if you would allow him to remain with us. I thank you for the friendship of this man. It's in your name I pray. Amen.

The bed creaked again. This time, Charlie definitely heard the squeak. He'd bet on it if he were a betting man.

Charlie's eyes shot open.

Blue steely grey ones stared back at him.

Behind the mask, Jack wore a smile that peeked out.

Now that Charlie's friend had woken up, he let out a deep breath. He rubbed the back of his neck. "You done scaring people?"

Jack eyes danced with the slight nod of his head.

The lopsided upward hook of Charlie's lips moved the same time his index finger circled over top him. "You know, I think you better talk to your doctor about GERD. Don't think those antacids are working."

Jack's eyes danced. A muffled chuckle squeezed out from underneath the seal of the oxygen mask.

A warning bell chimed. No lights flashed wildly, but the bell continued in a quick pace.

With the scan of Jack's bed, He saw nothing different from before Jack woke. But then he saw some movement at the side closest to him. A movement underneath the covers. He yanked the covers back.

A pulse oximetry lay an inch away from Jack's index finger.

Charlie swore under his breath. "Why can't they Velcro these on…"

He reached for the piece, but before he could grab it, someone with spry calloused fingers snatched it up and clamped it back onto Jack's finger.

The Chime stopped.

Charlie's head shot up.

An older lady, maybe in her seventies dressed with a red and white striped St. Agatha's Memorial Hospital volunteer smock with a tinge of blue hair smiled at Charlie then leaned toward Jack. "Oh my word, Jack, you causing trouble already?"

Jack winked at the new guest.

Another voice came from the foot of the bed. This time, a duplicate of who stood next to Charlie, but one wearing glasses. "Jack Barleyshot, what are you doing giving us all a scare like that?"

Charlie's head swung back to Jack. "You know these two?"

Jack's eyes danced.

Charlie rolled his eyes.

Oh Lord, have mercy on us.

"He sure does. He probably won't admit it, but in all reality, the man loves us."

A muffled laugh came from Jack.

Charlie studied the matching women. A few conversations played in the back of his head with Jack mentioning these two old birds and the mischief they got into. A smile peaked at the corner of his lips. He rubbed his jaw. "You wouldn't be the Antiquers would you?"

Both women smiled exactly the same. The one in glasses wiggled her fingers with his recognition. The other held out her hand. "We are. I'm Harriet Montgomery and this is my sister Hazel."

Unable to resist, Charlie shook Harriet's hand. "It's my pleasure."

Harriet glanced down at their hands locked together. She looked back over her shoulder to her sister. She held up Charlie's hand. "Wedding band. This one's taken."

Hazel frowned. Her fingers stopped wiggling. "Well no matter. He couldn't handle us anyway."

"And we only go for the untethered ones. Too much baggage otherwise."

Charlie laughed.

Jack laughed.

At that moment, a nurse popped into the room — the same twiggy-looking nurse from earlier. "Well, Mr. Barleyshot, it's nice to see you've woken up. I'll be back in a few minutes to check your vitals and give you your meds. SO don't go anywhere."

A low groan came from the bed, then a metallic squeak.

Charlie's eyes shifted back toward Jack. Unsure of what his best friend might be up to, he waited.

Hazel dug into her basket and held up a candy bar. "Here Jack, in case you get hungry." She wiggled the bar. "And it's dark chocolate too. That here is the good kind."

A smile crossed Charlie's face with those words. He actually chuckled to himself. These two old birds cared about his friend.

Nevertheless, from the corner of Charlie's eye, he noticed the shift in the bed covers as if someone were trying to move. He frowned.

He stared down at it. The bed lay with all white sheet and cover. Jack in between them of course, but not moving. Then the squeak sounded again. Charlie shifted to see Jack had successfully inched up on the bed.

Charlie narrowed his eyes. "Hold it partner, where do you think you're going?"

The faintest hint of pink tinged Jack's cheeks. He pointed a finger to himself and raised his eyebrows.

A scowl shot across Charlie's face. He stabbed a finger toward Jack. "Seriously? Yes, you. I don't talk to walls."

Jack smiled. He spoke through the mask. "Eight hours of no movement to my hip just might kill me. I think my sciatic nerve is acting up. I've got to shift positions."

Not going to let his friend bleed out on his watch, Charlie pushed down on Jack's shoulder. "Quit. Don't move. You want to make Lila a widow?"

After hearing those words, Jack's hands shot up. "Okay. But get me something. A muscle relaxer, painkiller, I don't care. At the moment, I don't care if I bleed out. But only for Lila, I won't if you do something about the pain."

Just then, the twig of a nurse returned with a tray of meds. "Mr. Barleyshot, how are you doing? Not moving I hope."

The women at the end of the bed giggled.

Hazel dropped the candy bar back into her basket all while she shook her head. "He might be dead before we get done with our shift."

Harriet slapped Hazel's forearm. "Oh Lordy, I don't give him that long."

Not one to pick on the sick, Charlie had a hard time not spilling the beans on him, but to save his friendship he bit back. "Can you give him something for his hip?"

The nurse dropped the little paper cup of meds. "Mr. Barleyshot, is there something wrong? You aren't bleeding out again are you?"

Jack shook his head. "No Ma'am. Just a little sciatica flaring up. I could use something to take the edge off. Either that or let me stand up."

A snort of laughter came from the end of the bed.

The nurse through her hands onto her hips and stomped a foot. "Mr. Barleyshot, are you trying to get me fired?"

"No Ma'am, but this will be extremely difficult to not move for eight hours with a sciatica flare-up."

The nurse grabbed his chart. "Let me see." She scanned the EMR with a few taps of the screen. "Looks like you can have some pain meds. I'll go let the doctor know."

As quick as she came into the room, she left, but not before pointing to Charlie, Watch him. If he moves that leg, hit the call button. I'll come in with some hog ties."

Charlie smiled. "It'll be my pleasure."

The nurse shot him a thumb's up. "I'll be right back." She pointed to Jack. "Don't move. Got it?"

Jack's jaw tightened. Everyone watching him could see the nerve jump in his jaw. The command made for a very unhappy Jack. A few curse words slipped past his clenched teeth.

Charlie chuckled to himself.

Hope that nurse moves fast.

Like a light switch, the nurse's order to lie still caused somewhat of a distraction. A distraction he watched his friend aim in the direction of the Antiquers.

Jack pulled the mask away from his face. "Ladies, good to see you."

Harriet moved next to Hazel. "Thank you Jack. And we are very happy that you're on the mend."

Charlie watched the banter go back and forth between the three. Disbelief of Jack's flirtation with the two after this procedure didn't surprise him. In fact, he expected it. It didn't offend most, in fact, Charlie could see that most were entertained by it and the two seventy-year-olds were no exception.

Jack cleared his throat. "What are you two doing here?"

Hazel held up a basket of books and magazines. "We volunteer to pass out reading material to the patients."

Harriet pointed at her sister and herself. "We help free up time for the nurses." She leaned over the foot of the bed. "Now we know you won't be reading anything for a while, but we wanted to make sure for ourselves you were okay."

Jack smiled. "I am."

Doubt crossed over the two's faces with Hazel raising an eyebrow over the rim of her glasses and Harriet giving him the eagle eye.

Charlie stood taller. He cleared his throat and glanced at the women, then to jack, and finally pointed to Jack's right hip. "I spoke with his doctor before I came in to see for myself. And he said as long as Jack doesn't move for the next eight hours, the femoral artery will heal up without needing surgery."

Harriet leaned into Hazel. "I hear that's what the sandbag is for. You know to put pressure on it so that artery closes."

Hazel nodded. "That's correct." She turned to Jack. "If you'd live a healthier lifestyle, then you wouldn't need an angioplasty."

Charlie chuckled.

Jack shot him a scowl.

The two women looked at each other then to Jack. "Count your blessings, young man. God did you a favor. Now don't waste it."

Jack smiled with a nod. "I don't plan to."

Harriet leaned into Hazel. "I told you God didn't want him yet."

In a stage whisper, Hazel leaned toward her sister. "That's right. The Lord's going to need every angel and probably old Lucifer to get him in heaven."

Charlie shook his head.

Heaven help him.

Hazel grabbed Jack's foot through the covers. "Well, then as long as you behave, we'll go finish our rounds."

Jack wiggled his toes. "By all means, please go."

Hazel and Harriet both gave Jack a wink.

Jack smiled. "Thanks for checking up on me ladies."

The two giggled.

Hazel pushed up on her glasses. "You get well now, you hear?"

Harriet turned to Charlie and pointed. "And you young man, make sure he doesn't move. He's still got things to do in Whiskey."

Harriet adjusted her basket. "You warn him if he doesn't behave, you'll tell Griff about all this."

Charlie frowned. He glanced at Jack who at the moment had his eyes closed.

Hmm? SO Griff is unaware of this little incident?

With that bit of information sinking in, Charlie's smile grew like the Rio Grande. Then as he glanced back to the two Antiquers, he gave them a two-finger salute. "Yes, Ma'am."

And on that note, the two bustled out of the room.

Charlie shook his head and chuckled. He turned to Jack. "I think they got a thing for you."

Jack lifted his mask. "They got a thing for my wallet."

Charlie's brow furrowed. "Your wallet?"

Jack nodded. "They think I'll fund all their projects."

"Don't you?"

Jack smiled that ornery smile of his. "No. I don't."

Charlie cocked his head. "If you don't, who does?"

Jack looked toward the door then back to Charlie. He pulled up on his mask. "Griff."

"Oh lord." Charlie shook his head. "That's going to get you into trouble with the man upstairs."

Jack smoothed down his blanket. "It's harmless. And anyway, those two there are the aunts of Griff's best friend. Their like family."

Charlie's eyes brightened. "That's a good thing. From what you've told me in the past, those two could be trouble."

Jack dropped his mask. "They are."

Charlie studied the man whose tanned skin appeared somewhat paler than usual. His eyes crinkled downward. He yawned.

"Tell you what, you've had enough excitement. How about I check up on you in a day or two."

Jack grabbed Charlie when his hand shot out. "No. I know you. And you want that info before I pass."

Charlie's brows arched. "Wow. Is that how you think of me?"

Jack dropped his hand. "Okay, maybe that's a little rough, but true. Remember I know you, Colonel."

Charlie took a step back. The temptation to pivot and exit crossed his mind, but he decided against it. Here Jack, his best friend, lay in a hospital bed where he almost bled out from a common procedure. He hadn't really thought it through on his mad dash to get to the hospital, but he had dropped everything and came. But why? He hated hospitals, well, actually not all hospitals, just ones that he helped carry dead soldiers into. So did he come just for the info?

After all, he and Jack had been through a lot over the years. So why did he ask this now?

Charlie rubbed the back of his neck. His muscles tightened, but no prickles. He dropped his hand and stepped back up to the bed. "You got a problem if I care what happens to your miserable hide?"

Jack's lips curled to one side. "Not at all. Just glad to hear you say it."

"I think those meds are messing with your brain."

Jack laughed. "Look here son, it's taken you nearly thirty years to realize the Military had all the Generals they wanted for now."

A little heat rose up Charlie's spine. "And?"

"And those of us who really care are glad your home. I honestly, don't believe you would have been happy there."

Charlie cocked his head.

The idea of living out the rest of his life in the military ran through his thoughts. And in all reality, the only thing he missed were the choppers. But, he had his own now. He could fly any time he wanted.

"You're probably right. And get that foolish idea out of your head, I came only for the info. In fact, I'll leave right now without it."

Jack laughed. "Hold up now. Let's not get dramatic."

"Dramatic?"

Jack waved his hand. "I got what I wanted. And now, —"

"Jack, just give me the info."

Jack leaned to his side, then back the other way. He groaned as he stared down at the sandbag on his upper thigh. "Old Scratch probably put that there himself."

Charlie shook his head. "You think he's got time for you?"

Jack shot Charlie a grin as he leaned to the side of the bed. "I reckon he's trying to torture me since my bleeding out didn't work."

Charlie braced a hand on Jack's shoulder. "Now, quit. You're not to be moving."

Jack blew out his breath. "Okay fine."

Charlie smiled. "You got anything?"

Jack adjusted his mask. "I'm pretty sure the clown's not getting out."

One of Charlie's eyebrows rose. "He's not? You sure about this?"

Jack nodded. Yes. He's not getting out

"I got a hold of Spence. Got him checking out the info on this parole hearing. But I've not heard back from him yet."

"He's getting quite slow in his old age."

Charlie laughed with that thought. After all, Spence had the best equipment out there. No one had any better, but maybe the government. And he also knew Spence had the stamina of a twenty-year old when it came to investigations even if he were in his late thirties.

Charlie circled a finger around Jack. "Yeah, said the spring chicken."

Jack smiled. "Oh spare me. Now did my contact call?"

"Your contact?"

"Okay, I'm guessing that's a no."

Charlie rubbed the back of his neck. "Not unless they've called while I was here."

"Well check."

"I will, but it'll have to wait until I recharge it. Phone is dead."

Jack nodded.

Charlie shifted.

Jack's brows rose. "Anything else?"

Charlie stopped moving. "Well, actually yes."

Jack pointed to the sandbag on his groin. "If you don't hurry it up, I'll pull this thing off myself. Now what else?"

Charlie leaned over on to the bedrail once more as his eyes danced. "You know anything about those clowns that Griff's put up at the shelter?"

Rather than Jack answering right away, Charlie watched his gaze drift toward the door then slowly come back to him. "Jack?"

"Did Josiah ever mention anything about helping out some old mules?"

"Mules?" Charlie glanced over at Jack's IV and pointed. "What are they giving you?"

A chuckle came from Jack. "Nothing good, because my sciatic nerve still hurts."

On those words, Charlie stared down at Jack. "You did hear me say clowns, right?"

"I'm not deaf."

"What do mules have to do with clowns?" Charlie tipped back his Stetson. "And if you say those clowns have them performing in that circus with them, then I'd say—"

Jack shook his head. He leaned to the side as far as he could. "No. Now listen." He shot a look over to the door. He then turned to Charlie. "These are Mexican mules."

Charlie's head fell backwards on Jack's words. He groaned. The tightness in his neck got worse. Almost immediately, his hand went to the sharp prickles forming.

He's got to be on something. That's all there is to it. I better give Griff a call and let him know about all this. Jack talking mules just might land him on the psychiatric floor if we're not careful.

Charlie's eyes closed as he tried to massage the tightness away. But the prickling snap intensified with each minute. He blew out his breath. "Mules? Seriously? Why would I care if they are donkeys?" *What do they have to do with these clowns?"

Jack smiled. This time, his smile cocked the oxygen mask up on one side of his face. "I did mention they were Mexican mules, right?"

With this declaration, Charlie's head wanted to explode. Jack made no sense at the moment. What in the heck, would he care about mules, yet alone Mexican ones?

Then as if a siren went off, it hit him.

Holy smokes.

Mules? Yes, he said mules. Charlie knew about Mexican mules. Anyone who flew choppers on the border of Texas and Mexico knew all about mules.

He smacked his head with his hand. His Stetson tumbled to the floor. "Are you telling me Josiah sheltered these Mexican mules?"

Jack said nothing, but the faintest hint of his cocked up lips on one side of his face lifted the mask making it just barely noticeable answered his question.

Charlie grasped the bedside rail. "Oh Lord," he waivered with huge eyes and his knuckles turned white.

The brows on Jack's face furrowed. He lifted up the corner of his oxygen mask. "What's wrong?"

"Evie. They're staying with Evie." And as those words spilled from Charlie's lips, he twisted to find his hat. The Stetson only lay a foot behind him. Charlie snatched it up and before he could shove it onto his head and leave, Jack grabbed his wrist.

"Hold up son."

Charlie jerked to a stop. "What do you mean hold up?"

Jack reeled his best friend closer to the bed. "Don't go all halfcocked. Griff's watching over her. And from what I found out, she's in no danger."

The air caught in Charlie's throat on those words. He searched Jack's face for the truth. "Are you positive?"

Jack nodded. "I am."

"How are you so sure?"

"Did you ever see the photograph Evie got from an anonymous admirer?"

Charlie's gut dropped as he shook his head. "Picture? What picture?"

"From what Griff tells me, Evie received an old picture of Josiah."

"And?"

"And it looks old. It's one with him on an island. But it could be fake. Just don't know these days."

"That doesn't sound good."

Jack laughed. "Don't worry. He's harmless."

"He? Harmless? Do you know this anonymous person?"

Jack laid back in his bed. A fairly sizeable twinkle danced in his eyes. "Yes. And you do too."

"What? Who is it?"

"Let me ask you this. Now, not including your chopper, what planes have you looked into buying?"

Wrinkles formed around Charlie's eyes as he searched his memory. He shook his head, not because he thought it would knock something loose, but because, he didn't fly planes. Helicopters were his thing. Not planes and especially not those little rickety things like he helped research for his brother-in-law seven years ago.

Charlie's chest tightened. The prickles on his neck stabbed at the back of his spine. And again, the realization hit him. "Holy smokes, are you telling me that picture is from Josiah?"

As a low chuckle eased its way out from behind Jack's mask, he gave him a thumb's up.

A low growl rolled out of Charlie's throat. "It's a good thing Susan declared him dead, because I'm going to hunt him down and kill him myself."

Jack's smile fell. He blew out his breath. The mask made a low whistling sound. "No my friend, not while I'm still alive. I don't visit anyone in prison."

Not thrilled with what his brother-in-law did, the words squeezed out from between Charlie's teeth. "Fine. I've got a better idea."

The bed squeaked again. Jack shifted to one side. "You going to let Susan know?"

Charlie's eyes danced. "Blazes, no, I won't torture him like that. And after all, he's given Evie her freedom. SO, no Susan." He rubbed his hands together. "But, I'll do worse."

The side of Jack's mouth curled up. "The clowns?"

Charlie rocked back in his boots. "Maybe."

"Maybe?"

"Yeah, I don't need you getting into any trouble with this."

"Trouble? When have you and I ever gotten into any trouble?"

Charlie scoffed. "Umm? Mogadishu? Germany? Basic training?"

Jack shook his head. "It's no wonder you didn't make General."

The words hit Charlie, but not like a boxer's blow, more like a pillow. In all reality, he thought, God must have had a plan for him other than the Military. Now he knew what he needed to do.

Save the family.

Text Message
May 11th
11:48 AM

Charlie: You got anything for me yet?

Spencer PI: Got the date and location of the parole hearing.

Charlie: Good. Send them to me ASAP.

Spencer PI: Also sent names and numbers via E-mail you'll need.

Charlie: That doesn't sound good.

Spencer PI: Depends on how you look at it.

Charlie: How so?

Spencer PI: Do you want him out or not?

Charlie: Gotcha.

Spencer PI: Anything else I can dig up I'll text.

Charlie: Sounds good, but need you to check something else out for me.

Spencer PI: Does it have anything to do with this clown?

Charlie: No. But does have to do with some other clowns.

Spencer PI: Seriously? You got a fetish for clowns?

Charlie: Excuse me?

Spencer PI: Sorry, Colonel, forgot the "LOL".

Charlie: Okay. Get me the name of those clowns staying at the shelter.

Spencer PI: Your daughter's shelter?

Charlie: Do you know of any other?

Spencer PI: How soon do you need it?

Charlie: Yesterday. And get me a number I can call one of them at.

Spencer PI: If they are staying at the shelter, can't you call Evie?

Charlie: No!

Spencer PI: Still keeping Susan out of the loop?

Charlie: Heck, yes. Someone's life might depend on it. Don't let her in on anything. Understand?

Spencer PI: Yes, Sir.

Chapter 12 Whiskey Breakfast

THE AROMA OF TOASTED SOUR DOUGH BREAD with the faintest hint of Smokey bacon and the rich brew of roasted coffee attacked Charlie's senses. His stomach growled. His head snapped up. He took in a deep breath and smiled.

Breakfast.

"If there's breakfast then there's coffee."

He pulled off his Stetson and tossed it on to a nearby bench. He flung open the door and in a quick cadence, he headed from the sunny mudroom where he normally stopped to rid himself of the evidence of him working out in the barn. The smell of coffee grew stronger.

His stomach growled again. Like a calf searching for his mammas utter, he headed straight for the table of food. Anyone who might run into him in the corridor, might think he resembled his prize bull that stopped for no one. And Charlie understood that for a fact. After all, when he herded the beast from its pen this morning, that's how he managed to get the current layer of dirt on his boots and hat. A dirt that fell into the streams of warm sunlight on the tiled floor. He brushed at his boots and jeans as he traveled down the hall. He shook his head. The dirt didn't want to come off.

He smiled at the thought even though his pride had lit up a notch or two because he proved to the young ranch hands he still had the moves and the smarts to get their most dangerous bull back into its pen.

Charlie halted. More scents of breakfast with aroma of fluffy buttermilk pancakes and scrambled eggs made his stomach ache with hunger. But the rich sent of the dark roasted coffee made him lick his lips. From the doorway, he searched the long oak table. His body froze. His gaze locked onto one spot. His coffee mug. Steam drifted upward.

Oh sweet heavenly father.

Charlie bee lined for the other end of the table.

"Ahem. Charles?"

Charlie groaned on the inside. He stopped. He ran a hand over his face.

Rats. Almost there.

He pivoted on one foot, took the few paces backwards, bent down to his wife and lifted her chin. "Good morning, Darlin'. Glad to see you up so early."

"Thank you Sweetheart."

Charlie leaned in and planted a soft kiss on her lips.

Susan smiled at first, but the longer his lips touched her's, she squirmed in her chair. "Charles, please my makeup."

Not wanting to let her go, he did only because his stomach growled. "Sorry, Darlin'."

As he released her, she grabbed for the San Antonio Express.

Charlie moved toward his end of the table and before he could sit down, Susan looked up from the morning paper. "Charles, did you finish with your chores?"

Charlie pulled out his chair and sat. "Got most of them done."

"And your calls?"

Charlie nodded. "Did most of those yesterday, Darlin. Just got one more to worry about."

"Good, then I take it that this will be the day Evie comes home?"

Charlie sank back against his seat with his stomach dropping. The corner of his mouth curled downward, as he closed his eyes. "What? Are you kidding me?"

Susan looked up from her plate. A smile pinched her lips. "Something wrong?"

Charlie pointed at his watch. "I've been out checking on the herd before the sun rose and you want to know what?"

Susan's face took on a splotched shade of pink. "Charles."

Charlie sighed. He closed his eyes. He'd hoped this discussion would take place on another day or not at all. But apparently, that wouldn't happen. He looked down at the full cup of hot coffee.

One drink before my appetites ruined.

He lifted the cup to his lips. He breathed in deep and long with his eyes drifting shut.

Susan growled. "Charles, don't tell me your letting her keep that good for nothing shelter to ruin our reputation?"

Before Charlie could take a drink, his eyes flew open. He slammed the cup to the table. Coffee splashed over the rim of his cup. A pool of the hot liquid started to run down the side of the table.

Susan squeaked.

He clamped his hands to the table and stiffened his back. "Susan, we talked about this already. I'm not doing this right now. I've got other matters more important to deal with than whose going to inherit Mae Foundation after you've died."

Susan gasped, "Charles."

"Well," he growled, "you aren't planning on retiring are you?"

The blotches of pink that stained Susan's face turned into a field of pink now. "But- but—"

He growled again. "Are you thinking about taking a spot in the family grave any time soon?"

Susan slammed her hand on the table. "Charles."

"Now listen here wife, you've got all the time in the world. Let Evie have this. She needs some happiness in her life. If she finds she's not cut out for it, then she'll come back."

Susan pushed the paper aside as her whole body went rigid. With Her face taught, a vein jumped in her neck. Teeth clenched cautious words passed over her lips. "But what about those clowns?"

"Oh hell, Susie, those clowns won't hurt her. They were friends of Josiah's. And anyway, Jack told me they were harmless."

Susan said nothing, but her glare set on Charlie told him he was right. A smile grew on his face, his tone softened. "I want whatever makes her happy. If running a shelter is that thing, then good for her."

"But—what—about—our—name?"

Charlie threw down his napkin and scooted back his chair. "Oh, for mercy's sake." He stood and pointed. "That little shelter is the last thing that would hurt our name. And so what if it did?"

Susan shot out of her chair. With one swipe of her hand, the creases in her grey skirt disappeared. "I can see I'll have to deal—"

Suddenly Charlie's cell phone rang.

He held up a hand then fumbled in his pocket. He tapped the screen once he had hold of the phone. He blew out his breath. "I've got to take this."

"But I'm not done."

Charlie glared at her. "But I am."

Susan pivoted on her three-inch matching grey heels. "Charles. I'm not done—"

Charlie tapped the screen, held the phone up to his ear with one hand and waved Susan off with the other as he walked out of the room. "Hello you old son of a gun, it's been awhile. Jack said you might call. Is that state house still standing?"

Text Message
May 13th
10:02 AM

Charlie: How you feeling?
Jack: As good as my horse.
Charlie: Didn't your horse die a year ago?
Jack: And your point?
Charlie: Being a little over dramatic aren't you?
Jack: Hunger doesn't make for happiness.
Charlie: Lila got you on that rabbit food now?
Jack: How'd you guess?
Charlie: Let's just say your horse is nicer than you right now.
JACK: He's dead.
Charlie: And you will be too if you don't change your diet.
Jack: Just shut up. Now tell me what you want.
Charlie: Meeting with Spence later.
Jack: And?
Charlie: He's got some info for me on the mules.
Jack: What's next?
Charlie: Working on a plan now.
Jack: Have you told Susan yet?
Charlie: Seriously? I'm not crazy.
Jack: You still haven't told her?
Charlie: Just because you don't mind dying, doesn't mean everyone else
              feels the same.
Jack: Wow! Nothing like a friend to stab you in the heart. Huh?
Charlie: IF it means lassoing truth around you, I will.
Jack: Let me ask you this, you got your will prepared?
Charlie: Yes. And you better get yours ready. Because if Susan
finds out, I know who to look for.
Jack: Already done.
Charlie: Your friend called.
Jack: And?

Charlie: He informed me that "no way in everlasting fire" would any convicts be paroled before they served their minimum.

Jack: You still going to the hearing?

Charlie: Possibly. First need to talk to Spence.

Jack: Need a driver?

Charlie: No. Don't need to get you involved any more than you are.

Jack: What's the fun in all of this then?

Charlie: My witty conversation.

Jack: This is texting. Technically, we're not conversing.

Charlie: Go eat a salad!

Chapter 13 Whiskey Investigation

WITH SKIMPY GRAY CLOUDS HOLDING DOWN THE SKYLINE, Charlie leaned forward with hands resting on his truck's steering wheel. The truck carried a number of miles on it, but he had no intention of retiring it soon. But at times, he wished the digital panel on the dashboard could accommodate magnification, especially when the work of ranch life tired him out and now to add the stress of this whole clown thing made him a bit more tired.

He shook his head as he leaned closer to the digital clock. "Come on Spence, I don't have all day." He licked his bottom lip.

As he glanced back out the window, the spot he parked near had some traffic on the sidewalks, but why wouldn't it? The truck sat halfway between the library entrance and a coffee shop.

He rubbed his jaw. He could see the old English stencil letters etched across the large picture windows that spelled out Beans and Leaves. A few rod-iron café tables with red and white striped candy cane umbrellas dotted the street with matching chairs and cushions.

That there looks like the coffee shop that twig of a nurse mentioned.

His mouth felt a little dry. After all, he hadn't had anything to drink since lunchtime. Maybe he'd get himself a cup, better yet, maybe one of those fancy double shots of expresso he heard his cowhands talking about on early mornings out riding to check the fence lines. If Spence didn't come soon he just might do that.

A burst of laughter and squeals broke his thoughts on the coffee when a few children tumbled out of the library up ahead of him. They playfully stood at the curb. A little girl with reddish-brown curls waved at him.

Friendly thing.

Charlie waved his fingers in salutation. The little girl's curls jiggled as she threw a hand over her mouth. She poked the boy next to her who turned to look at Charlie. He stuck his tongue out at him.

Charlie chuckled to himself then stuck a thumb up.

The boy grabbed the little girl's hand and skipped across the street just as a dark sedan with blacked out windows slowed behind them.

Charlie watched the newcomer. The sedan slowed, almost stopping to allow for any other kids to follow the boy and girl. Once they were in no danger of being hit, the car passed Charlie's truck and made a U-turn. The black sedan pulled up behind Charlie and parked. Charlie watched for signs of life from the car. But no one got out.

He glanced at the dashboard. His arrangement to meet Spence on the hour had arrived and with the car behind him, all mysterious looking with its darkened windows and black color put him a little on edge. After all, the whole thing with the clowns had its own mysteriousness about it. The idea of someone wanting to let the prison clown out sooner than the minimum stuck in his craw. And now, Evie also had to deal with some homeless troupe of clowns. Sure, they might be nice. But they were friends of Josiah's. And possibly Mexican Mules. Had Josiah's plane really crashed? The thought of it didn't sit well in his brain. After all, he'd been the one to find that Cessna for him. He wouldn't steer family toward something that would kill them. He loved flying his choppers and he knew Josiah liked flying too. Sure Josiah didn't fly every day as he did while in the military, but the man did manage to collect the hours to fly keeping his license current. So what happened?

Charlie shrugged his shoulders and mumbled to himself. "Guess will never know, but maybe, just maybe…"

A flash of lights flickered into the rear view mirror.

Charlie's eyebrows rose. He shifted in his seat to get a better look.

He narrowed his gaze on the car now parked almost bumper-to-bumper behind him. He couldn't recall a vehicle like this belonging to Spence. SO who dared such an act?

Charlie pulled off his sunglasses. Sunglasses he usually wore everywhere, but at the moment the graying skimpy clouds transformed into heavy dark ones whose shadow now cast over three car lengths.

With his fingers tightening around the steering wheel, he twisted back into his seat and glanced at the clock. Another ten minutes had passed. No other car appeared that one might find his friend Spence driving. And even though the fondness of the mysterious car behind him made him curious, it held no sway in prompting him to figure out who had the nerve to park directly on his bumper. Yes, he might have done it ten years ago, but now, he wouldn't risk it. He'd seen the reports about people and their road rage. He might have been crazy enough at one time to fly choppers into a battlefield, but he'd been prepared to die for his country then. But now? He shook his head. Well, Charlie knew the Lord had saved him for something and figured if he wanted him up there in heaven he would have taken him out their when he flew through all the bullets and rockets. Him getting out to confront someone because they'd flashed their lights at him and sat on his bumper did not mean God wanted him now.

Charlie closed his eyes for a second. The idea of Evie reopening the shelter filtered into his thoughts.

Good Lord, has Evie put herself in danger? Is that why I'm still around?

This worry, shot spikey tingles of pain down his neck to his tailbone. He rolled his shoulders.

A light tap on the window popped open his eyes.

His head snapped toward the sound. Someone stood at the passenger door. The tap came again.

A muffled "Colonel, it's LTC. Open up before the rain hits."

With the air backed into his throat, Charlie finally breathed out when his finger hit the lock switch and popped the lock up.

Large raindrops slid between the newcomer and the truck. A well-toned man who had at least two inches on Charlie slid in-between the door and the rest of the rain.

Charlie hadn't seen Spence in quite some time, but the guy had a toned muscular frame just like his friend. The glasses that the man wore slid down his nose. Amber colored eyes stared over the rim.

The tension in Charlie's neck faded.

A hint of a quirk to Charlie's lips curled on one side. "Okay, Spence so now you've taken to driving sedans?"

An almost exact hitch of Charlie's lips rose on one side of Spence's mouth.

Spence chuckled as he started to climb into the passenger seat.

Charlie snatched his Stetson and stuffed it haphazardly onto his head.

Spence pulled the door shut.

The rain came down harder.

"Let's just say it's a loaner for now."

An eyebrow rose on Charlie's forehead. "A loaner, huh?"

Spence's grin dimmed.

"So Colonel, you want that news on your clowns?"

Charlie gave a curt nod. "And don't call them my clowns."

Spence's quirk of a smile returned. And without hesitation, he reached into the inner chest pocket of the black nylon jacket he wore. "Well, Colonel, I've got some good news and some bad news." He held up a hand. "But, I'll let you figure out which is which."

Charlie's head swiveled ninety degrees. His gaze narrowed on the PI.

No grins or chuckles came from Spence when he declared this. His neck tightened. The prickles along his spine hovered over his skin ready to stampede across his back. He let out a slow breath and tried to relax in his seat with a clear mind. But that rotten clown from thirty years ago danced across his thoughts. His teeth sank into the inside of his cheek. He sat back against his seat and looking out into the street ahead of him he braced himself for the information Spence dug up. With his fingers white knuckling the steering wheel, he nodded. "Okay, let's have it."

Spence pulled out a stuffed envelope and tossed it onto the console. "Those there are some of the shelter clowns."

Charlie glanced down.

"The Mexican cartel has a bounty out for them."

Charlie's gaze shot toward the PI. "What for?"

Spence fingered another envelope he pulled out, but did not hand it over. "Their mules."

"But what about the bounty?"

"They're mules gone astray."

Charlie cocked his head. "Astray?"

Spence nodded.

Charlie noticed his glasses slipped a bit down his nose.

"Yeah. Seems they got sick of what they were doing. And decided a few years ago they needed to get out."

"A few years ago?"

Spence's lips quirked again to one side. "Okay, maybe about twelve years ago if you want specifics."

Charlie tipped back his Stetson. "I do."

"They got tired of all the transporting of the children to the States and them being turned into dealers or worse—"

"Or worse?"

Spence blew out his breath and shifted in his seat. He stared out the passenger window. "Ever hear those stories about kids being trafficked?"

Charlie said nothing. He knew all about them. Susan had told him how a few times over the years they found stray kids wandering their pastures. And he also knew from patrolling the borders that kids were involved. But he'd always hoped those were just political rumors to stir up the masses.

"Well, their true. And sick of it, they decided to get their families out of Mexico so no harm would come to them. "

Charlie turned in his seat. "Did they get them out?"

Spence nodded. "They did. But it cost them a lot."

Charlie's neck grew tighter. He breathed in a few deep breaths. "And?"

"Well, apparently your brother-in-law used his shelter as like one of those in the Underground Railroad."

Charlie's eyes widened. "Josiah?"

Spence nodded again. "He befriended that troupe a long time ago. In fact for many years, the Cartel had no clue as to where they were losing their money, drugs, and quarry."

"So how did they find out?"

Spence rubbed at his jaw, then turned back to Charlie. "Either someone ratted them out or the Cartel realized their return didn't match up to what they figured they should get."

Charlie let out a low whistle. He stared down at the envelope of pictures. "And Josiah?"

"Well, my sources say, he bought an island somewhere and hid the clowns and their families."

Charlie raised his head to his friend. "But why are they hear now? Why wouldn't they be on this island too?"

Spence shrugged. "Haven't figured that one out yet."

Charlie rubbed the back of his neck. Thoughts raced through his mind.

Why would they be at the shelter? They'd have to know the cartel would look for them. And why would Josiah put Evie in danger? How would he know how to protect her?

Anger rose in his chest. Clenching his jaw, not wanting to take the frustration he had for his so-called dead brother-in-law out on his friend he held back the temptation to yell. "Okay, what about the other? You know, the birthday clown?"

Spence held up the other envelope. "Here's a copy of a letter."

"A letter? To who?"

"Your birthday clown."

Charlie growled with narrowed eyes. "Look here." He pointed. "I won't say it again—"

Spence winced. "Okay. Sorry." He waved the envelope. "The question should be who sent the letter and why."

Charlie snatched the envelope from Spence's hand and tore it open. He scrutinized the page once he'd unfolded it. Shock and anger ran through his head. The prickles hovering over his neck broke free like a wild bull penned up at the rodeo trying to throw a cowboy from its back. He crumpled the letter in one fist and growled. "It's a good thing he's been declared dead, because when I get my hands on him, no one will miss him."

Text Message
May 16th
6:10 AM

Charlie: Darlin', might be home late.

Susan: Might?

Charlie: Need to fly out to Midland. Should be home before the storm hits. Getting ready now to leave.

Susan: Midland? What's in Midland? Or should I ask who is in Midland?

Charlie: Maybe it's a boot designer.

Susan: You're buying your cattle boots now?

Charlie: Funny.

Susan: Have you fixed things with Evie?

Charlie: Refresh my memory… what do I have to fix?

Susan: Charles.

Charlie: No, but I might talk to her soon.

Susan: Soon? What have you been waiting for?

Charlie: I told you I've been working on other important things.

Susan: What things?

Charlie: Business.

Susan: You're going to Midland? Right?

Charlie: Yes. I'll be home tonight. We can discuss it then.

Susan: I thought you were going for business?

Charlie: Yes.

Susan: I'll ask one last time, what business and why do you need to talk to me about it?

Charlie: We'll discuss it tonight.

Susan: Charles, I'd appreciate honesty.
What aren't you telling me?
Does this have to do with Evie?

Charlie: If I tell you now it'll ruin the surprise.

Susan: I don't care for surprises.

Charlie: Not even if there a pair of those hand crafted leather Italian boots you've been wanting?

Susan: Are they?

Charlie: Now Darlin' if I tell you it will ruin the surprise.

Susan: You're impossible.

Charlie: But you love me anyway.

Charlie: Susan?

Susan: Size 7.

Chapter 14 Whiskey Parole

WHERE CHARLIE SAT, THE AIR AROUND HIM GREW HEAVY. Maybe heavy from the storm moving across the state from the coast, but more than likely the heaviness came from the circumstances, which brought him to his present location. A location he never figured he would ever visit. And the fact that none of these such places across the state used air conditioners only reminded him of the brutalness of the whole situation.

So, yes, Charlie understood what the circumstances would entail today. And they still didn't deter him from coming. In fact, Charlie had visited a place or two like this when he served in Afghanistan. He knew what coming to the Texas Federal Penitentiary would entail, but never did he visit a place like this where he had some sort of an emotional connection to it. Nor did he know anyone personally while in the Military that caused him to visit. But here in the states, that fact didn't hold water. Charlie knew of only one person from his past that might invoke a visit. And unfortunately, with the matters at hand, he now waited to see that person. This person created no sincere thoughts within his ticker. Maybe long ago, if he'd met this particular man on the streets and found him down on his luck, but he hadn't. Instead, this man had done the one thing that made his heart rage. And kidnapping his daughter at the age of eight left a mark on his heart as if someone had branded him those twenty some years ago with nothing, but anger. Anger that rarely anyone ever saw. And at the moment, this hate within him stirred deep inside. Right now, angry nerves danced under his skin. So sitting in the visitor's room waiting to talk to his daughter's kidnapper at the Federal penitentiary would allow any person in his inner circle a glimpse of that anger. But like the Colonel, he used to be, Charlie kept his feelings under wrap. No sense in making a display of himself. Because he knew that would be counterproductive. He mentally tightened up on the reigns to this encounter and as he'd come for information that he might not find the answers anywhere else. So, keeping his cool would be vital.

He glanced up at the clock, with only minutes away from the kidnapping clown's appearance, Charlie took in a few deep breaths to clear his thoughts, but most of all to tamper down the raging nerves that roiled underneath his skin. Charlie let the last deep breath of air slip past his lips. More at ease, but not wanting to look as though this meeting held no importance, he grabbed for his brown Stetson off the empty metal chair next to him and put it on. In doing so, he had no intention of showing this man any kind of courtesy. He came for answers and nothing but answers.

After straightening the Stetson, he sat taller and waited. And as if putting on his hat cued the visitation time to begin, Charlie's ears perked at the low sound of rubber-soled shoes shuffling across the cemented floor.

About time.

About time.

Not wanting the other man to figure out what this all meant to Charlie, he pulled his Aviators from his pocket and slipped them over his nose. With only a few seconds before the man would sit across from him, Charlie offered up a prayer. Not just any prayer, but one that would help with his temper, but mostly one for answers. Never did he expect to be sitting here, but with the whole thing on the clowns at the shelter and Evie now owning it, plus not to mention the info that Spence dug up, he just had to get the truth. And why not get it from this man. After all, he had a connection to everyone involved.

Lord, give me the strength to deal with this man calmly and without hate. I know he's doing his time, but please don't allow him to think in any way I'm here to help…

The drag of metal raked across the cement floor with the sound of a cable following in its wake.

But, Lord, if he's willing to help, I might find it in my heart to say a few words at his parole hearing, but only if you will it. Amen.

Eyes open now, Charlie focused on the man that stood behind the chair. He pointed for him to sit. He studied the man who finally gave a short nod and sat down.

In all reality, the man looked nothing like the cocky punk clown who'd kidnapped his eight-year-old daughter almost twenty years ago. In fact, this guy had wrinkles that strained against the corner of his lips and eyes. His skin no longer had afresh tinge of sunshine to it, but instead it held a slight grey cast to it like the clouds that the weather forecast predicted for later in the day. Even the edges of his hair around his sideburns entertained the gray. Granted the aged eighteen-year-old once had eyes that danced with angered energy from what he could remember in the courtroom some twenty years ago, but these eyes were now tinged toward the pulpy insides of a lemon — pale yellow. And their movement could only remind him of a listless cloud on a hot day in Texas.

Charlie held tight to a cringe that wanted to spread across his face, but instead let his stomach take a few rolls. But the cringe hadn't been compassion for him. No, he hadn't been able to work himself up to any feeling like that. But, on the inside, he cringed at the proof of what hard time did for a man who would serve time, forty plus years to be exact if one didn't make parole. And on that note, Charlie shook the pity off for what amount of time any criminal might have to serve. After all, he believed if you did the crime, then you did the time. No ifs, ands, or buts about it. And with that philosophy, Charlie wanted to remind this clown, he'd do what he could to make sure he served at least the minimum if not all of his sentence. And why not, he stole his daughters trust and security from her. Not anything that one could easily get back either. And this infuriated him.

Charlie had no intention to making anything easy on the man, so he waited for the silence to prompt the clown into speaking first.

And in a low gravelly tone, he did, but from what Charlie could guess only after checking for extra ears because the man said nothing until he'd glanced over both shoulders about a half-dozen times.

"You wanted to see me?"

Charlie nodded.

"About what?"

Charlie crossed his arms over his chest and stared at the clown. After studying the man for a long heartbeat, Charlie cocked an eyebrow enough so that it peaked over the rim of his aviators. "Rumor says you're getting paroled soon."

Not much of a reaction to this news came from the clown. Only a slight tilt upward from the corner of his lips did Charlie notice. And in return, he slowly shook his head with his own lopsided grin.

The clown's smirk disappeared with his eyes wide. "*Que?*"

Charlies grin stretched more. "I said nothing."

"But your head. You shook it." He leaned closer. "*Dime?* What do you know? Tell me."

Charlie crossed his arms. "I don't recall saying anything like that."

The clown searched the little cubicle before he sat back into his metal chair. "Then why did you come?"

Charlie dropped his arms and leaned into the bulletproof shield. "I'm here to let you know, criminals, like you, should do their full time. All of their time. Because it's easier on everyone."

The clown sat up. The smirk slowly returned to his lips. "Everyone? You mean your daughter?" He licked his lips. "She's twenty now, *sí?*"

The anger that cautiously danced on Charlie's nerves now pooled at the base of his spine and readied itself to explode like a shotgun he'd use on any pack of coyotes stalking his heard. His fingers gripped the edges of his chair and dug in. His voice lowered to a growl. "Look here son, you don't know who you're messing with."

The clown gulped, but instead of using any sensible thinking, he egged Charlie on further. "A redhead, *no?*"

Charlie gritted his teeth as he pulled back and dug into his coat. His examination of the man never strayed. The visible sweat forming at the clown's hairline grew more evident as one bead of sweat rolled down the side of his face. Charlie pulled out a folded sheet of paper. One that looked suspiciously like the sheet he'd crumpled between his fingers after Spence had given it to him. He slowly unfolded it, then turning the printed side to the clown, he pressed it up against the window. The hook to one side of Charlie's lips returned. "You recognize this?"

The clown ignored the paper. He looked straight past it. "You think you—"

Through clenched teeth, Charlie growled. "Stop. Read it." He pointed to the paper.

The clown leaned in. His lips moved without words passing over them. He jerked back into his chair causing it to rock backward. His gaze darted back and forth from the paper to Charlie. "How did you get that?"

Charlie pulled the sheet away and with his phone, he tucked both back into his coat pocket. "So you understand now, why you should finish out your time?"

The clown's shoulder's fell. "You won't let anyone know then?"

Charlie nodded. "I won't, but tell me this Do you know Juan Carlos?"

The clown glanced over his shoulders then leaned in and gave the faintest nod. "*Sí.*"

Charlie inched up on his seat. "How?"

"*Es l hermanno de mamá*"

"Your mama's Brother?"

The clown nodded. "He gave me the info."

Charlie's eyes widened behind his glasses. He bit down on his jaw to keep it from falling onto the floor. His fingers curled into fists. "Brother? That's it. I am going to murder that SOB."

The clown jumped from his seat. His fist made contact with the bulletproof glass. "*No. No.* But what about my *mamá?*"

Charlie stood. He slid his chair back. He took his time after all, he wanted to make this clown understand who had all the control. At no point in time, would he allow this clown to think he'd relinquish any control. "I hear some prisoner's families do real well if everyone plays by the law and doesn't ride out on favorites. Then I guess there isn't much to worry about. Correct?"

The clown's face fell as he slumped into his chair. A low groan slipped out. His hands raked through his hair. "*Jijo de —*"

Charlie shook his head as he backed out of the cubicle. "Once I talk to Juan Carlos, you shouldn't have to worry about your mamá. Just remember statistics say early parolees usually end up back in prison, so it's best to do your minimum. Right?"

Miguel hunched over in his chair. The man looked quite small now. Not frail, but defeated. He finally nodded. "But what about the *gringo?*"

Charlie cocked an eyebrow. He stepped closer. "Who?"

Miguel slowly looked up at Charlie. "The *gringo*. She has the *gringo*."

"What *gringo?*"

"The whiskey *gringo*."

Charlie rubbed at his jaw now not sure what to make of the man's words. "What's this *gringo* supposed to do?"

Miguel's eyes brightened. He sat up. "You don't know of the whiskey *gringo?*"

Not wanting Miguel to have the upper hand, Charlie stepped closer pushing his own chair up to the wall and leaned forward. "Son, I know everything about this whiskey *gringo*. So don't be trying to play games with me." He pointed a finger at him. "I know lots of people."

Miguel slumped back in his chair with eyes closed. A few words crossed over his lips, but nothing anyone standing there could interpret. And anyway, he had no intention of letting this man play mind games with him.

Positive he got what he wanted with this visit and uninterested in deciphering the kidnapper's mumblings, he turned to exit.

Stupid fool.

But before his thoughts became vocal, he bounced back slightly. Caught off guard, Charlie's one eyebrow had arched almost swallowed up by his Stetson. Still pretty spry on his feet, he managed to keep ahold of his hat so as to prevent it from colliding with two men who appeared out of nowhere. As his hand fell away from the brim of his hat, he scrutinized the two men.

One stocky and wore glasses, the other well toned with a crew cut. Both in suits and had dark hair to boot. Plus he noticed on each of their lapels a small pin that resembled the Mexican flag.

Hmm? Odd.

Charlie gave the men another once over. The men didn't appear to be anyone he knew, but they did remind him of someone, but who?

Not able to recall who the two looked like, he stepped back to let them squeeze into the cubicle. "Let me get out of your way. I'm done here. He's all yours."

The slightest hint of a smile appeared on the stocky gentleman.

The loud scrape of chair legs broke the three men's concentration. Each of their heads snapped to the spot Miguel had sat only a minute ago. Charlie tipped back his hat where the other two men displayed frowns.

"Sorry about that. Hope it's nothing I did."

The stockier older man nodded as if he knew Charlie had nothing to do with Miguel's disappearance. But the other man, the younger one, grunted in disbelief that the seat across from them had once been filled. Now, no one remained there. "Well blazes. We don't have time for these games."

Charlie had started for the exit, but on those words, he halted and took a look over his shoulder.

Hmm?

The two men were correct. Miguel had vanished. But, why? Who were these two to him? And who were these two men after all? Dark suits, Military-styled haircuts, and the pins on their lapels. The questions ran around in his head. But still he couldn't figure out who they were. Maybe because he had such little time. Maybe if he could actually talk to them longer. But at the moment, he needed to keep moving and the man deserved no more special attention, after all, he did kidnap his daughter twenty some years ago.

He shook his head. Unable to figure it out, he pushed on, besides, he had his own problems to deal with. But then suddenly an image slipped into his view. Nothing too specific or anyone in direct contact to today, but something prompted him to understand with the way the guys were dressed meant a lot more to the whole situation than he originally thought.

Charlie jerked to a stop. "What? Federales?" He glanced over his shoulder, but the two men were on their cell phones. Words in rapid-fire Spanish drifted toward him.

A bit of curiosity prompted him to reach for his own phone. But he halted pulling it out.

"Crap, I knew I should have downloaded that translator app when Evie mentioned it to me."

He shook it off. "Just forget about it. There's bigger fish to fry at the moment." Then with that thought, another one sprang into his head.

Whiskey gringo? Who is this whiskey gringo?

Text Message
May 20th
6:40 AM

Charlie: Humphrey, old man, you back from apple picking yet?

Humphrey: Good afternoon. And no. I stayed an extra week.

Charlie: How soon will it be before your back?

Humphrey: What can I help you with. I did bring my laptop.

Charlie: Fantastic. Can you draw me up two cashier's checks?

Humphrey: Two?

Charlie: Yes. Two. One for Evie and one for a Troup of Clowns.

Humphrey: So you don't need my services to freeze Evie's account then?

Charlie: At the moment no. Just need the checks.

Humphrey: Okay. I believe I understand the one for Evie, but the clowns?

Charlie: Trust me. It's a worthwhile expenditure.

Humphrey: Is this coming from you and Susan's account?

Charlie: No. And I would appreciate you avoiding any phone calls from Susan that might come your way.

Humphrey: Charlie?

Charlie: Can't explain right now. But don't worry, it's all legal.

Humphrey: You know, you could do this yourself.

Charlie: Don't have time. And I want it done right.

Humphrey: Okay, if you say so. I'll need some info.

Charlie: Send me an E-mail of what you need.

Humphrey: How soon do you need it?

Charlie: How soon can you get it?

Humphrey: You sure you want to do this?

Charlie: At the moment, I'm afraid it's my only option.

Humphrey: How should I record this?

Charlie: Soon as I get that info, I'll let you know.

Humphrey: Very well. I'll wait for your E-mail.

Charlie: Don't worry, it's nothing worse than what Josiah would do.

Humphrey: Josiah Westerfield?
Charlie: That's the one.
Humphrey: But I heard he was dead.
Charlie: We better hope so.
Humphrey: Charlie?
Charlie: Loosen up. It's a joke. This though is for a good cause.
Humphrey: I'll wait for the details.
Charlie: Good man, Humph. Enjoy the apples.

Chapter 15 Whiskey Clowns

A SUGARY LEMON FRAGRANCE PERFUMED the air within the chilly breeze that swirled around Charlie. The sun not at its full zenith didn't help with the unusual coolness to this time of late spring, but Whiskey, Texas didn't sit too far from the Gulf Coast so in all reality the temperatures could dip at times when the Gulf decided to stir things up.

Charlie rubbed at the goose bumps forming on the back of his neck. Another waft of the chill in the air circled around him. He tapped on the top of his Stetson to secure its spot on his head. His nose crinkled as he stared straight ahead of him. The dryness to his mouth had his eyes on a quest for a cup of coffee. But no such luck. Only one thing he could find and he had no taste for it at the moment. Coffee, cold or hot did not matter to him. He loved the stuff. Actually, that and Barleyshot Whiskey, but that refreshment he couldn't drink on a daily basis. Well, not if he wanted to get anything done that day. And the drink trailer that stood in front of him in the shape of a lemon made his stomach sour.

Not today. But coffee, that's a different story.

With a slight shake of his head, he pressed on, but not for coffee. He actually searched for the one thorn or more like a group of thorns in his daughter's side and with the help of Spence, he managed to secure the location where he'd find the culprits -- the little ragtag group known as the Banzoff Circus, specifically the troupe of clowns.

Charlie patted at his breast pocket. A crinkling of paper came from within his jacket. He gave a nod to himself. Not that the nod signaled that the papers were still within his jacket, but more like for what the papers were for. His mission today would be to secure some peace for his daughter. Ever since the kidnapping, twenty some years ago, Charlie drew on a strength of protectiveness for Evie and his wife. He'd do anything for their safety. Hence, Sam, the retired Navy Seal and chauffeur that he's employed since the day the authorities rescued her. And not to forget their housekeeper, Lucia who came to work for the Stockton's almost immediately after the whole incident. Thanks to Charlie and his connections, Susan never suspected the petite athletic-looking woman to have previously worked for Special Forces.

He smiled to himself. With his marriage to Susan, he rarely had the chance to put one over on her. Not for lack of trying though, but more because Susan knew him so well. After all, they'd married thirty plus years ago and they were high school sweethearts on top of that. So, getting something past her took some work. But luckily, for him, Lucia worked. Of course, Susan knew Sam came from the Seals, but as far as Charlie knew, his wife knew nothing of Lucia's Military service.

Charlie loved his wife, but sometimes her opinions and ideas of who or what people should do drove him nuts. That's why she never suspected Lucia as being anything, but their housekeeper. After all, Susan, didn't believe women should join the military. She always told him they were more important than hauling around weapons and playing war. No, Susan believed women were a lot stronger than men, not in physical strength, but in intelligence and resourcefulness.

So when Lucia's last tour ended, Charlie made her a sweeter deal with working for him by taking on the role as housekeeper and undercover bodyguard. He knew Susan would hate the idea of having one for herself, hence the secret.

Charlie let his hand drop. The envelopes remained in his inside coat pocket. The tension in his shoulders lessened. He scanned the path in front of him. A few other food trailers had their windows open and smells of spicy sausage, greasy French fries, sweet cotton candy, and roasted peanuts reached out to him as he stepped past them.

His stomach grumbled. He unclipped his phone from his leather belt. One tap to the screen lit it up. The clock app came into view first.

Almost noon, hopefully they aren't at lunch.

Charlie pushed the phone back into the clip and glanced back down the fairway. A curl to his lip turned up one side of his mouth. He strode forward on the somewhat trampled grass and headed for the destination that lay in front of him. The shape of the structure appeared familiar, but not the color. Most structures like this entertained their guests with one or two colors, but not this one. In fact, it hosted a whole rainbow of colors. But then again, what else might a circus dress their big top in to attract attention.

Charlie shook his head and pulled his glasses from his nose and stuffed them in a pocket. Not a fan of circuses, he rolled his eyes at the vibrant colors. Now rodeos, those were different. More his style. He needed nothing of what a circus needed to draw in a crowd. Just have some broncos and bulls with the top rodeo riders and he had no need for fancy colors or attractions. But then a thought hit him.

Both have clowns.

His stomach tightened. His brain tried to push the connection away from his thoughts.

Why after all these years had I never correlated the two?

He shook his head as if he were a bronco trying to shake off its rider. Nothing though. The image of a rodeo clown stood next to a circus clown. He rubbed at his forehead.

Remember, they look nothing like each other, except for some paint on their faces and one saves lives, not destroys them.

Charlie nodded with that reasoning, but his heart had a different thought on it. And with a twinge to his chest, it reminded him good clowns versus evil ones couldn't compare. For instance rodeo clowns were clowns too, which helped dominate the good ones…

A burst of Calliope music broke Charlie free of this internal debate.

With his hands now on his waist, he blew out his breath. He stepped forward with an ornery quirk to his lips.

Okay. Let's figure out just who they are. The good ones or the bad ones.

He approached the entrance where the door flap hung down with one strip of the material tied to the side panel. He yanked on the tie and pushed through as darkness within the tent pulled him forward.

With only the thin beam of sunlight chasing after him, he paused inside the tent. His crooked smile melted into a frown.

Under his breath, he growled.

Oh for the love of all mighty. Where are they? Spence said they'd be here.

He searched the tent. No one but bleachers and a makeshift-gated area where handicapped circus goers sat. He pulled his phone from the clip once more and swiped at the screen. He shifted from one booted foot to the other.

Maybe Spence said one and not noon. After all, most people ate at noon.

Then without warning twinkle lights appeared as if stars lit up the sky just after dusk.

Charlie's arm dropped to his side. His fingers dug into his phone. He slowly scanned the tent. Lights lit up almost every surface -- the poles, the sides, the ceiling, and even the ring that walled off the onlookers from the performers.

Charlie cocked his head. A faint rustle of Calliope notes drifted toward him. Not sure of what might happen next, he stepped back to the entrance he came through and waited.

Thoughts of an elephant or tiger appearing made prickled hairs stand up on the back of his neck. He licked his lips. He continued to search for the next clues, but nothing. No one appeared at that moment. Charlie let out the breath he didn't realize he'd sucked in when the twinkle lights flicked on. He stuffed his phone into his pocket once again and tipped back the brim of his Stetson.

Now with one hand at the back of his neck, he rubbed at the prickles. "Okay, now what?"

Then suddenly with a burst of the Calliope music at stadium level and the twinkle lights now flashing wildly in no specific pattern, an irritating bleating honk came from the other side.

Charlie's eyes grew wide. He backed into the tent wall.

Straight ahead of him on the opposite side of the big top a large white star surrounded by a rainbow circle decorated that part of the canvas. Then as if someone ripped a piece of industrial-strength Velcro from the wall a large rip of fabric in the middle of the white star echoed under the big top. The bleating honk came in rapid succession, but not loud enough to drown out the Calliope notes, which danced out from the speakers attached to the two-story poles holding the big top in place. The zip of an engine and a streak of bright blue metal with colored spots flashed past him. Grass clippings and dirt puffed up in the vehicles wake.

Charlie closed his eyes to try and steady his breathing. For the most part he never thought about his health, but with this incident, he now understood his daughter's worries about sheltering a troupe of clowns.

The bubble of a car screeched to a stop. The Calliope music changed to a faster pace. The creak of something metal swinging open enticed Charlie to look out at the ring. One -by-one, clowns of all sizes and shapes exited the back of the car. About five in total not including the miniature poodle that wore his own colorful dress that sat on one clown's shoulder who wore a flowerpot for a hat until a sixth one, the last one, popped out.

Charlie gaze narrowed on this one. This clown had the height and build on him like no other clown he'd seen at a circus. This one moved gracefully around the car with stealth as each limb showcased each muscle through the rainbow-colored suit that clung to every inch of his body.

His lips started to curl once he recognized the makeup pattern they wore.

Definitely not circus clown style, but rodeo. Now that's a different story.

Charlie watched on as one clown pulled bowling pins from the back seat of the car and start juggling them. Another one blew bubbles at a make believe crowd, the third one pulled a unicycle from the trunk of the car and climbed on and wheeled himself around the ring tossing out what looked to be flower petals. The forth one wore a flowerpot hat and carried a hula hoop out in front of him signaling with a whistle for the miniature poodle to do a series of jumps and flips in and around the hoop, and the fifth one wearing large red floppy shoes bounced around on a pogo stick that tooted. Finally, the sixth one, the rainbow-suited clown smiled out to the ghost of a crowd and waived as he turned on his heels. Once he managed to rotate in Charlie's direction his movement faltered. The clown's arm fell to the side of his hip matching his other one. He leaned forward as if to get a closer look at Charlie. One eyebrow rose as he cocked his head.

Then as quick as the excitement had started it halted with the crack of the snap of his fingers.

The twinkle lights halted their dance around the tent. The Calliope notes faded to a dull low, and the other clowns stopped what they were doing and gathered behind the rainbow-suited clown.

Charlie straightened his hat and stepped a foot closer. He cleared his throat. The lack of getting himself something to drink earlier popped into his thoughts along with the lemon shaped shakeup stand he passed only minutes ago. Mentally, he shook off the thirst.

Just get this over with, then get a coffee.

Just get this over with, then get a coffee.

He took a few more steps.

The clowns moved as one. Now less than half way between them, the rainbow clown held up his hand signaling to the others to stop. He then stepped away from the troupe. A large grin spread over the clowns face.

Charlie pointed at the rainbow suited clown. "Are you, Juan Carlos?"

The rainbow-suited clown's smile faltered for one second. Then it went back to its usual brightness. He nodded. "*Sí*. And you are Charlie Stockton, *no?*"

One of Charlie's eyebrows almost disappeared under the brim of his Stetson. He dipped his brim in acknowledgement. "I am."

Charlie stepped up to the rainbow-suited clown. A two-foot barrier wall with stars glittering on its sides stood between them. "I understand you're staying at the Whiskey Salvation Shelter."

Juan Carlos' smile returned. "*Sí.*"

"I reckon you know my relationship to the owner then?"

Juan Carlos nodded with his smile even larger.

Charlie adjusted his weight to his other foot. "Then you're probably wondering why I'm here."

Juan Carlos' brows knitted together. The smile on his face dimmed, but didn't disappear altogether.

Charlie studied the man. Although he had the size of a professional wrestler and looked as if he could toss cattle out of his way if they crossed his path, the man still oozed a genuine sincerity about him. After all, who wouldn't wearing the colorful suit he had on. But at the moment, Charlie would admit that the man's smile no longer presented itself with all of his questioning. Not wanting to make this an all-day-event, Charlie got straight to the point.

"I understand you used to know Josiah Westerfield real good. Is this correct?"

Juan Carlos' lips curled up at the corners.

But to Charlie's disappointment, no verbal confirmation came. Charlie blew out his breath as he rubbed at his forehead. "Look, I don't care if you're friends."

One of Juan Carlo's eyebrows rose looking as if it were ready to spill over his forehead.

"Since I got the right clown troupe, I'd like to offer some assistance."

Juan Carlos cocked his head. "Assistance? But what makes you think we need assistance?"

"How about the fact that you and your band of merriment worked for a certain Cartel and helped them deliver their product until you met Josiah about some years back."

Juan Carlos licked his lips. He shifted from one foot to the other.

Not sure what the clown seemed to be doing, but to Charlie it looked as if a hint of worry crossed this giant clown's face. The hairs on his neck tingled.

The small group of clowns started to murmur in Spanish.

Juan Carlos finally settled, but not before holding up his finger to silence his fellow clowns.

The mumbles died down.

"*Sí, señor.* This is true."

"Good."

Now both Juan Carlos' eyebrows arched. "*Bien?*"

Charlie nodded. He tipped back his Stetson then placed both hands on his waist pushing back his jacket. "I've got a proposition you might want to seriously consider."

Juan Carlos cocked his head studying Charlie. After a long minute, he signaled for him to continue. "Explain."

"Word on the street is that the Cartel is looking for you and your friends."

The troupe of clowns gasped.

Juan Carlos glanced over his shoulder while holding up a finger to shush his friends. He shook his head.

Charlie studied the other clowns. Even though he walked in on what looked to be their practicing their routine, they did wear their pancake thick makeup, a makeup that usually hid everything. But not this time. No this time they wore their makeup like the rodeo clowns did with only parts of their faces covered by the traditional makeup. Unfortunately for them, wearing it like rodeo clowns do, it allowed for a real human look with their mouths hanging open and eyes bulging as if they would pop out of their sockets.

A slight twinge hit Charlie in the chest. Not a twinge of pain, but one that made him feel for the clowns, which in all reality Charlie would deny to his dying days. But after what he gathered from Spence, he realized this troupe of clowns were actually some of the good guys, not just good clowns, but actual good guys. One's he'd consider wearing white hats.

Charlie held up a hand. "Okay, hold on now. Don't get excited. I'm not here to cause any problems. I'm actually here to help you out."

The little troupe curled around Juan Carlos tighter. Each one of their painted faces started to take on a look of surprise. But not Juan Carlos. Instead of surprise on his face like the others whose brows rose and mouths dropped open, he crossed his arms over his chest and waited. His dark brown eyes glared at Charlie.

Charlie's head dipped in acknowledgment of Juan's suspicion of his intentions. But not to be deterred by this, Charlie reached into the breast pocket of his coat and slowly pulled out an envelope. An envelope that had the name San Antonio National Bank on it.

Charlie stepped closer to Juan and held out the envelope.

Juan Carlos didn't budge. In fact, the man waited with crossed arms.

Charlie remained in his spot positive that this clown and his troupe were not happy with the mention of the Cartel, but to Charlie that didn't matter to him. No, at this moment, the only thing that mattered took on the responsibility he had to his wife and daughter. He promised both of them, no matter where he laid his head at night whether in the Army or back home on the ranch, they would always be safe under his watch.

Determined to make this clown thing go away for once and for all, he inched the envelope out to Juan Carlos. "Take it, you won't be sorry."

For a long moment, the rainbow-suited clown narrowed his gaze. He shifted on his feet then looked at each of his clown buddies. One-by-one, they each nodded their head. Juan Carlos in return nodded back to them. He reached out with one white-gloved hand and started to slide his fingers down the edge of the envelope. But at that instant, the hairs on Charlie's neck tingled. Two words popped in his head that he hadn't been able to shake for the past few days.

Whiskey gringo.

And since Juan Carlos and Miguel were family and they were all tied up in this whole fiasco in one way or another, Charlie had the gumption inquire about the kidnapper's incoherent ramblings.

Charlie pulled back the envelope slightly and held up a finger. "Hold on a minute. Before I give you this, I need to know something."

Juan Carlos' slowly drew back his hand allowing his arm to fall to his side. A slight curve to his lips pulled at the corner of his mouth. "*Sí?*"

Charlie rocked back on the heels of his boots as he tipped back his hat. "I met a friend of your families the other day."

Juan Carlos head dipped. "And?"

"I'm at a loss. He mentioned someone to me. I'd like to know if you know him and how it relates to this whole situation."

Juan Carlos' eyes brightened. The troupe of clowns leaned closer. A low murmur hummed around the group.

Charlie cocked an eyebrow in their direction. "Is it safe to talk in front of them."

Juan Carlos again folded his arms over his chest and nodded. "*Sí.*"

Charlie rubbed at the back of his neck. The prickly tingles still danced under his skin, but not as though it were spurs digging into it. He held up the envelope again. "You know anything about some whiskey *gringo?*"

The low hum circled the small troupe, but grew with more animation and volume. Finally, Juan Carlos snapped his fingers.

The crack reverberated off the big top's walls. The clowns quieted.

Juan took a step closer. "*Sí*. I know this Whiskey *gringo*."

Charlie arched an eyebrow in the rainbow suited clowns direction. "And?"

"He is an old friend." Juan Carlos circled his finger in the direction of his troupe. "We have known him for many years."

Charlie licked his lips. "Does he work for the circus?"

Juan Carlos shook his head. "No he rode the circuit."

The word circuit danced in Charlie's head for a moment when the image of a bull scattered it. He rubbed his jaw. "A rodeo cowboy then?"

Juan shook his head. "*No Señor* Charlie, not a rodeo cowboy anymore."

Tired of the guessing game and the slight pounding of his temples, Charlie blew out his breath as his shoulders fell. "For heaven's sake man, I don't have all day. Who?"

Juan Carlos smiled as he clapped his hands twice. The small troupe of clowns raced about gathering their props and scurried into the little car. Juan Carlos stepped away from Charlie, circled the front end, and when he reached the driver's door he opened it. With one hand on the roof he stopped himself before climbing in. "*Señor* Charlie, let me ask you this, who has the best whiskey in town?"

Charlie's gut tightened. He thrust his hands to his waist with narrowed eyes on the rainbow-suited clown and his car. "Now wait a minute. Stop playing games with me. After what I've brought you," he held up the envelope now crushed under his fingers. "You won't tell me who this whiskey *gringo* is?"

Juan Carlos chuckled. "You sound as though you need a drink. Why not try some whiskey?"

Charlie growled. "Look here you son of a—"

Juan Carlos held up his hand. "I will meet you for coffee in a few days. Just think about this whiskey *gringo*. It will come to you. If not, I will introduce him to you. *Sí*?"

Charlie closed his eyes. The envelopes in his hands crumpled into a wad of wrinkles. He counted to ten to prevent himself from doing anything drastic. And before he had finished and opened his eyes, Juan Carlos climbed into the car, tooted the horn and sped out through the Velcro ripped open white star.

Charlie kicked the two-foot wall in front of him and growled. "Curses on you, Josiah. If I ever get my hands on you, you'll wish I hadn't."

Text Message
May 22nd
4:45 PM

Charlie: How you holding up?

Evie: Well, that depends.

Charlie: Really? On what?

Evie: Are we talking about the staff I need or the clowns?

Charlie: Clowns? You still got clowns there?

Evie: Yes. Traveling circus clowns. Their fifth wheel broke down.

Charlie: Any trouble out of them?

Evie: Not really, but they don't like my cooking.

Evie: Daddy?

Charlie: Hold on. I'm speechless.

Evie: That's not funny.

Charlie: Do you have your insurance paid up?

Charlie: Evie?

Evie: Good question. Another thing to put on my list.

Charlie: Good God girl. What are you thinking?

Evie: I'm thinking I need a cook and an office assistant.

Charlie: Can you afford them?

Evie: I believe so. But another reason to get an assistant.

Charlie: Want me to send your Mamma to help?

Evie: Daddy. That's not funny.

Charlie: Sorry. Just wanted to lighten the mood.

Evie: Thanks. But she'd never come anyway.

Charlie: Now Evie, she does miss you. In fact, she asks me every day when you're coming back.

Evie: Does she?

Charlie: Yes, she does. You really should give her a call.

Evie: Last time we talked she accused me of trying to sabotage Mae Foundation.

Charlie: I'm sure she didn't mean it that way.

Evie: Mother has a control issue.

Charlie: Yes, she's quite stubborn. I know someone else who is that
            way too.
Evie: That's not fair, Daddy.
Charlie: Stubbornness aside, she only wants the best for you.
Evie: Then she needs to let me have a life.
Charlie: And that's at the shelter?
Evie: Yes.
Charlie: Need a cup of coffee. Let me know if you need help … with
            the clowns, alright?
Evie: Can I hire Lucia?
Charlie: No! Put an ad in the Gazette.

Chapter 16 Whiskey Cowboys

"WHAT THE–"

A streak of blonde blew past the front of Charlie's truck.

He stomped on the brakes. The tires squealed. Burnt rubber filled the air. The truck rocked to a stop.

His phone crashed against the front window and then tumbled off the dashboard.

A shot of adrenalin made his heart kick like a bronco. Just to make sure no hooves popped out of his chest he stuck his hand inside his coat to double check. His breathing slowed as he stared after the dasher. With the blinking of his eyes, a hand shot up and he heard the melodic sound of an apology drift back to him.

Only for a second did he wonder if this felt the same as a heart attack. He'd have to ask Jack next time he talked to him just to be on the safe side, after all, heart attacks at his age were not unusual.

More questions tried to break into his thoughts, but a car horn tooted behind him.

Charlie glanced out his rear view mirror and realized his truck now blocked traffic. He held up a hand signaling to the driver behind him he would move. And fortunately for him, he spotted an open along the curb to pull over. Once stopped, Charlie threw the gear into park. Not sure where his phone fell, he pulled off his aviators and reached over to the passenger side floorboard. Unable to find it immediately, he realize it had slid under the seat. He groped around for it.

As he blew out his breath, he dug further under the passenger seat. His fingers grazed the phone. He shifted for a better angle. At that moment, his fingers curled around the phone where he then pushed himself back up.

Now that he had found his phone, he reminded himself that he had two things to accomplish. One get a cup of coffee and two, figure out how to get rid of the clowns.

But in all reality, it didn't matter which came first. More times than not, did the first thing make problems for him. So coffee topped the list today.

After adjusting his sunglasses, he peered out the window and scanned the location he had parked at. Fortunately for Charlie, he found himself pulled along the curb next to the coffee shop — Beans and Leaves. He smiled to himself.

Now with his phone secure in his pocket he grabbed his keys from the ignition and climbed out of the driver's seat.

The traffic on the street had pretty much disappeared. Well, enough for him to observe the going ons over at the Whiskey Salvation Shelter. Yes, the building lay in the middle of the square, but with Charlie's eagle eyesight he had little trouble with seeing distances. In fact his eye doctor at his last visit couldn't believe at the age of fifty plus, he still had ten-twenty vision. Charlie remembered telling the eye doc it ran in the family. But he frowned at that thought. He shook his head.

No. Evie doesn't have it.

Charlie blew out his breath and shrugged.

Not like she needs it.

A high-pitched voice carried over the square.

Charlie snapped out of his thoughts and focused on the direction of the voices. He tugged on his sunglasses just enough to see two women arguing. One stood on the front steps of the Whiskey Salvation Shelter. The woman's wavy blonde strands of hair fell from the clip holding it up and swirled just above her shoulders. Her hands waved in a frantic motion. The other with auburn-colored hair stood eye-to-eye in her black riding boots in front of the animated woman and shook her head.

Charlie narrowed his vision on them. He tipped back his hat and let out a chuckle. "There's my girl." He studied the other woman. He rubbed at his jaw and mumbled through his fingers. "Hmm? That there looks like Evie's friend. Now, what's her name?"

An image filtered into his head. No more like a newspaper article. Actually an article in the San Antonio Gazette's sports section. A snapshot of a much smaller pixie-like young girl held up a medal. The caption underneath shouted out -- State Bound! Margo Brooks breaks the hundred -yard dash record by two seconds!

Charlie's smile widened. "Margo Brooks."

Evie and Margo went way back. In fact all the way to kindergarten. Charlie always liked his daughter's friend. She held no grudge against Evie for what happened at her eighth birthday party. Not that Evie had anything to do with Susan cancelling the rest of the event once they found Evie missing. Nope, not once had Margo abandoned Evie's friendship, even if it meant that no matter where they traveled a bodyguard followed. So for this reason, Charlie figured it one of their little spats. He'd let them handle it. But maybe after he got his coffee and spoke to Juan Carlos, he'd surprise them with a box of fudge. After all, the fudge came highly recommended by the Whiskey Community Hospital's nursing staff.

Charlie's curiosity held on for another second. Unfortunately, one second too long though.

Thwack.

Charlie rocked backwards. His hat fell to the side.

Bells echoed around him. The scent of coffee rushed forward. His The forward momentum that carried Charlie forward waivered.

He stumbled back. The heel of his boot tipped down on the edge of the curb. His eyes went wide. He reached out for what he bumped into to hopefully save him from the fall, but instead, a calloused pair of hands grabbed him and hauled him back upright.

"Got ya old timer."

The man who prevented Charlie's crash hauled him back on the sidewalk a few feet and steadied him.

Charlie straightened his now skewed sunglasses. From the corner of his eye, he spotted his hat and bent for it.

Old-timer?

Now with his hat back on and his glasses straightened he took a good look at the cowboy.

To his surprise a grin flashed across the cowboys face.

Not one hundred percent sure who stood in front of him, he pulled down his sunglasses. The cowboy took a step backwards. Charlie studied him. He wore a black Stetson, jeans, some sort of sport coat, and a decent pair of Western heritage boots. Not that Charlie knew everyone buy their clothes, because all cowboys wore jeans, boots, and a sturdy hat, but what confirmed the identity of this cowboy had to be those piercing green eyes, black as coal hair, and a familiar cocky grin, plus not to mention that blasted toothpick that hung from his mouth.

Charlie chuckled. "You know, one of these days you're going to swallow that thing."

On those words, the other cowboy smiled. "Not today." He pulled it out from between his lips. The twig of a stick hung together by a sliver. "But you could be right, one of these days I just might."

Charlie's hand shot out. "How's it going Griff? It's been a long time."

The younger cowboy grabbed Charlie's hand and pulled him in for a hug. "It's going pretty good."

When Griff released his hold, Charlie noticed the slight distraction in the man's sunglasses. He examined them for a second. He spotted Evie and Margo in the reflection. He also noted a hint of a frown pulling on the corner of Griff's mouth.

Charlie shifted in his boots as something stirred in his memory. Jack's voice slowly whispered from his thoughts.

Griff's seeing Evie.

The scuff of the boot heels brought the younger cowboy's full attention back to Charlie.

"Sorry about that. And you?"

Now with total recall of that conversation, Charlie's protective mode kicked up a notch. He hadn't expected to see Evie so soon and with what looked like more problems at the shelter and possibly Griff's involvement, his neck tightened. With an arched eyebrow, he threw his thumb over his shoulder. "You sorry for the collision or the mess over at the shelter?"

The corners of Griff's mouth turned down. He tipped back his Stetson. His hands went to his beltline. He rocked back in his boots.

"You here to tell me to stop seeing your daughter?"

Charlie looked Griff up and down. The tone of his voice hardened. "Is there a reason I shouldn't?"

Griff stuffed the broken toothpick into one of his coat pockets. He glanced over toward the shelter and blew out his breath. "She recently found out my connection to Jack."

On Griff's words the conversation with Juan Carlos rode into his thoughts.

Jack? Griff? Jack? Whiskey?

Charlie tugged on his sunglasses and peered over the tops of them. He studied him for a long minute. The flash of a young Griff wearing leather chaps dusting himself off with his hat after he'd managed to get thrown off a bull at eight seconds of riding sashayed across his memory. Charlie grinned.

Whiskey gringo?

Griff cleared his throat. "Charlie you okay?"

With the shake of his head, Charlie snapped back to the present. "And?"

"She also knows I'm on the committee that wants the shelter."

"And?"

Griff rolled his eyes. "Come on Charlie."

"Anyone ever call you whiskey *gringo*?"

A red tinge crawled up Griff's neck. "Where'd you hear that from?"

Charlie adjusted his aviators. "Never mind that. So she's realized you're a jack ass?"

Griff pinched the bridge of his nose. "I wouldn't say quite that."

Charlie's eyebrows rose. "Then what would you call it?"

Griff shrugged.

Not happy with the news, Charlie crossed his arms over his chest. "You explain your situation?"

Griff blew out his breath.

Charlie said nothing, he just waited. He knew the boy. And eventually he'd explain.

In all reality, it had been quite some time since their paths crossed. But Jack made sure to keep him updated on the matters when it came to his nephew. And why not? Jack didn't have any kids of his own, and when Jack's brother-in-law got himself killed in the rodeo long ago, Jack took on the responsibility of helping raise him. And with Charlie and Jack being best friends, well that meant, Charlie would help out too.

Griff stared across the street. His voice lowered to a mumble. "Not yet. But I did tell her in not so many words that I had no plans to help the mayor acquire the shelter."

With jaw tightening Griff's words -in not so many words-" strained to pass Charlie's teeth. "Boy, you sure don't have the communication skills I thought your Mamma raised you with some sense."

Griff's head swung back to Charlie with huge wet eyes. His mouth hung open enough to make one think he had a reply, but instead, his chin hit his chest with one hand disappearing under the brim of his hat.

Charlie swore to himself. He shook his head with his gut taking a nosedive.

You, Charlie are a fool.

Not sure what to do, he did the only thing he could. He stepped up to Griff and wrapped his arm around him pulling him into a hug. He felt the weight of Griff slump just a little. He hugged him harder. Leaning closer for only Griff's ears. "I'm sorry son. I didn't mean to say that. Your mamma was one of the best and I know how hard it was for her to raise you after your pa died."

Charlie squeezed harder. "Hell, if there's anyone to blame for lack of communication, I blame it on Jack. That old cuss wanted the property himself and didn't bother telling me."

An almost inaudible sniff came from Griff's direction.

Charlie loosened his grip.

Griff's shoulder rose.

Charlie understood the signal. Loyalty went far here in these parts.

Griff agreed with Charlie, but would never voice it.

Charlie dropped his arms and stepped back. "So if there's anyone to blame I lay it all in his lap."

With the hem of his coat sleeve, Griff took a swipe at his eyes then adjusted his Stetson. "Jack should have told you his intentions. But I'm an idiot for not being upfront with Evie."

Charlie studied Griff. He watched him glance over at the shelter.

Griff turned to Charlie. "I don't know why I didn't tell her."

Charlie pointed to Griff's chest. "Sounds like the ticker's been doing most of your thinking these past few weeks."

The corner of Griff's mouth lifted. "Yeh. I know. And I don't think I can stop it."

Charlie laughed. "No boy, that's for sure. Once you find that special one your ticker and the thinking is her's."

Griff's brows rose.

Charlie tapped on his chest. "I'll vouch for it. In fact I bet a bottle of Jack's best that his Lila's done the same to him."

Griff's smile got larger. "Sorry, but that's one wager I won't take."

A stunted jingle of bells from over at the coffee shop broke Charlie's attention. He shifted to see Juan Carlos standing halfway out the door. The rainbow-suited clown held up a coffee.

Not ready to end the conversation, Charlie caught Juan Carlos' eyes and silently nodded.

Juan Carlos took a drink from the coffee he held then as the pure enjoyment of the coffee appeared on his face he slowly saluted with the Styrofoam cup and turned back into the coffee shop.

Charlie's taste buds moaned as he licked his lips.

The crinkle of the plastic that encased a fresh toothpick Griff pulled from his coat brought him back to their conversation. Charlie frowned. His stomach tightened. In the Army, he had a whole team to plan out their missions, here he had himself. He thought at first Susan wanted the best for Evie, but the longer she stayed away, the more difficult and demanding Susan got. Now with this new problem, the one here with Griff, Charlie hadn't the faintest clue, but to tell the boy to follow his heart. Most times it didn't steer him wrong. After all, he had the track record to prove it with his marriage to Susan for the past thirty or so years. He'd be the first to admit it, things didn't always go his way, but for the most part it did. And this time, in order to get some peace in the family he needed to help Evie, but not do it in a way that Susan would ever find out and leave him.

He examined Griff from the heels of his boots to the top of his Stetson. He nodded to himself.

Evie needs a good man in her life and Griff just might do, if the boy gets his act together. And why not help him? Plus, if he resolved the whole clown issue Susan would no longer have anything to hold onto to keep Evie from living her own life. Right? Then again if Susan ever found out his plans she might string him up.

He sighed and threw up a quick request

Lord, need some help here.

Nothing came to Charlie. He wanted to hand the whole matter over to Susan, but she wanted Evie to have no part in Jack's family. But she didn't know Jack like he did. And without Griff's pa, Jack had stepped up and helped raise the boy.

The local Methodist's church bells rang.

Charlie's brows furrowed. He stepped closer to Griff and lowered his voice. "Best thing to do right now is help her in any way you can—"

"But I think she'd rather stick me with a pitchfork right about now."

Charlie grinned. "She wouldn't be a Stockton if she didn't stick you once or twice."

Griff's eyebrows furrowed. "Anything you want to tell me about your daughter that I should know that might save my life one day?"

Charlie's smile got wider. "Just that she's a lot like her Mamma in looks, smarts, and attitude."

A low whistle fell from Griff's lips. He rocked back on his boot heels. "I've read those articles featured in all the business magazines. If she's a lot like her Mamma, then I got my work cut out for me."

The smile disappeared from Charlie's face. A more serious tone came from his words now. "Don't matter, just do what you can. Doesn't mean you need her permission. Just do it. And if you have to, for Lord's sake, one way or another tell her."

Griff nodded then pulled out his sunglasses. "Good to have you back here in Whiskey."

Charlie laughed. "Well, son, if I don't get my part of this fixed, I may just be reenlisting."

Griff's head cocked to the side. "Reenlisting? Seriously?"

His eyes danced. "Would they take an old cowboy like you back?"

Charlie rubbed at the back of his neck. He smiled. "If this don't work out like I want it to, they better."

"Or?"

"Or I'll wish I'd bought a chopper that could fly more than 400 miles on one tank."

The Methodist church bells quieted. Only a few cars drove on the street in front of them. A car door shut, then the chirp of a key faab sang out. A woman carrying a stack of books hurried into the library situated next to the coffee shop.

Unaware of the time until the church bells went off, Charlie pulled out his phone to check it. A deep scowl settled over his face. The tap to the screen confirmed the time. He needed to get going or he'd lose his time with Juan Carlos. But before he could say anything to Griff, he noticed the mischievous twinkle in his eyes.

Oh good gravy. I've seen that before.

Charlie had to admit, he hadn't ever seen the look on Griff before, but Jack definitely. He gulped. His neck muscles grew a little more tighter with his next words.

"What?"

Griff chuckled. "Now don't throw a shoe. What I got in store just might rid us of half our trouble."

Charlie cocked an eyebrow. "Okay, I'm listening."

Griff pointed towards the shelter.

Charlie twisted to follow his finger.

Five clowns had gathered out front. One wearing a flowerpot hat with what looked like a small black dog stood at one side, another with red shoes blew bubbles from a harmonica, another with a colorful wig rode around in circles on a unicycle, while one stood on his hands inside a hula-hoop with balloons tied to his feet, and the fifth who wore a unicorn headband juggled something that looked to be a lot like melons.

"How about you lending a hand with the clowns."

Charlie looked upward.

Lord, you're not helping me out here. This isn't exactly the signal I expected.

No trumpet of horns, no locusts or flash floods came. Nothing. Frustrated that God wanted him to work this one out on his own, Charlie blew out his breath. A headache rooted itself just above his brows. He pulled just enough on his aviators to massage the most sharp point. With his teeth clenched he shot Griff a look. "In what way?"

"Well, their nice clowns, but I think Evie would really appreciate them out of her hair."

Charlie nodded. "And just how do you figure I can help?"

Griff smiled as he pulled the toothpick from the corner of his mouth. "Didn't you just mention you got a chopper that flies four-hundred miles on one tank?"

It took only a second for what Griff suggested to register. With another second, he made a whiplash movement of his neck to spot the rainbow-suited clown's profile smiling as he sat at the table near the front window holding a cup of coffee. Charlie's gut clenched. The blood vessels near the spot of the headache pulsated with what resembled a heard of longhorns thundering down a canyon. Once the words finally settled, he growled.

"Now hold on here boy, you aren't serious?"

Charlie: Darlin'? Everything okay?

Susan: That all depends.

Charlie: Should I even ask?

Susan: Oh sure, don't ask. Chicken.

Charlie: Now hold on hear. I apologize. I know you don't like to be teased.

Susan: Brilliant deduction.

Charlie: But you are quite cute when you get riled.

Susan: Any of those medical doctors ever think to check your brain after all the years you spent in service?

Charlie: They did, got a clean bill of health when I retired.

Susan: Ha!

Charlie: How can I help?

Susan: My campaign's falling apart.

Charlie: The Million Dollar Lady?

Susan: Yes.

Charlie: Trouble with your star?

Susan: Grrr. Don't mention that woman's name.

Charlie: Okay.

Susan: She refuses to do any more photoshoots unless we change the makeup.

Charlie: All of them?

Susan: Yes. She says she looks like a clown.

Charlie: Speaking of clowns. I believe our trouble with a certain birthday clown will no longer be any trouble to us.

Susan: Oh really? Is he up for parole? Is it that time already?

Charlie: Yes.

Susan: That Elizabeth Gardner has me so frazzled. I can't believe I forgot about the parole hearing.

Charlie: Don't worry. I took care of it.

Susan: How?

Charlie: Never you mind, it's a man thing.

Susan: Grrr? You're impossible. You know I'll eventually find out, don't you?

Charlie: I talked to Evie.

Susan: You're changing the subject.

Charlie: She's doing fine now.

Susan: Now? What happened?

Charlie: Let's just say some unexpected friends dropped in at the shelter and stayed a while.

Susan: Does this mean she wants to sell it.

Susan: She's realized running a shelter is beneath her?

Charlie: Susan. That's our daughter you're talking about.

Susan: One can hope can't they?

Charlie: I've told you before, she's more of a social doer than a business doer.

Susan: The boots came.

Charlie: Boots?

Susan: Didn't you order me a pair of boots?

Charlie: Nice distraction.

Susan: Learned from the master.

Charlie: Now quit buttering me up.

Susan: Is it working?

Charlie: Possibly.

Susan: Good then order me the matching purse.

Charlie: Love ya, Darlin'.

Susan: I know.

Charlie: Finish up that campaign and lets you and I go somewhere.

Susan: Somewhere?

Charlie: Yes, Ma'am. Bell will be ready to go soon as you can get away.

Susan: Tomorrow?

Charlie: Well, maybe not that soon. But how about this weekend?

Susan: Why not tomorrow?

Charlie: I need to make a quick flight to Dallas.

Susan: For what?

Charlie: That purse, right?

Susan: One of these day's Colonel, I'll figure out just exactly what
            you're doing.
Charlie: Do you want the clutch or over the shoulder handbag?
Susan: Grrr?
Susan: Both!
Charlie: Love you Darlin'.
Susan: Love you more.

Chapter 17 Whiskey Chopper

WITH ONE HAND ON THE CYCLIC CONTROL STICK, Charlie took his other to tug down on his aviators. His dark brown eyes peered out over the nose of his Bell helicopter. A blue sky with puffy white clouds dotted the skyline. He chewed on his bottom lip when he spotted off in the distance the dark clouds that rolled behind the others. He glanced down at the instrument panel. He gave it a quick nod. All the gauges met his approval for the speed and height of the chopper. He pushed on the stick and pressed the yaw pedals that allowed the twenty-two hundred pound black and silver bell jet ranger to climb higher into the sky.

The blue sky and a light wind of about five knots came to no comfort to him. Not even the puffy white clouds that hung over the horizon helped, which always reminded him of the fluffy pillows Susan stacked on their bed. He pushed up on his aviators. The pressure building from his front temporal region dug in. Not a surprise to him either. After all, the battle going on in his head right now some would consider D-day, which he personally considered it as do or die day. And although the day might not be as precarious as some missions he'd flown, this one he figured no less the dangerous. Okay that might be a stretch physically, but mentally, it did not compare. Especially with the cargo he would deliver to the Dallas Ft Worth helipad. After all, his marriage just might depend on the success of this hop and not to forget, the safety of his daughter too.

The chopper hummed with the rotation of the blades above. Charlie's heart and lungs fell into sync with the steadiness of the flight. The bell climbed another five thousand feet and leveled out into a path clear of any of God's birds or other mechanical ones. He blew out his breath and eased back on the stick. Time need not be of the essence to him at the moment, just getting to the Dallas Executive helipad intact however held the top spot on his mental list of importance, but he did want to land before the storm brewing ahead of him hit Dallas at the same time he made his descent. If need be he could always fly over it and circle back, but he figured the cargo in back probably wouldn't take too kindly of another ascent, not especially if he couldn't block any weather communications broadcasted by the tower the closer he flew to the landing pad.

Lord, please hold off on that storm for a bit longer. Let me get this load to RBD before it hits. Otherwise you might be welcoming in a whole bunch of us this afternoon. I thank ya for obliging. Amen

Charlie pressed on the stick.

The chopper's engines whined. The metal bird crossed the skyline with great speed and agility, but in all honesty that talent came from the many years Charlie had flown in the Army. Normally, he did not miss those days, but today it had cross his mind once or twice. And in those times, he could and would fire against the enemy if engaged. But now that he had retired, engaging the enemy did not appear as one of his choices no matter how much they might tempt him. So instead, he clenched his jaw and held his tongue, and most of all, he kept his hands on the stick. He groaned to himself. The unnecessary chatter bouncing from one headset to another made him wish he'd never offered up the microphoned earphones, but instead he wished he'd passed out the noise cancelling ones. Others though, just might agree that this little disturbance would be worth it, but only, if it resolved the issue. Charlie, himself understood the events of the day wouldn't make everyone happy. But if he didn't divulge everything then he figured no harm, no foul. Right? He rolled his eyes, but not long enough that it would distract him from the dark clouds that formed on the horizon. For the most part, the sky hosted the puffy white clouds, but again those dark angry ones looked to be moving in faster than he liked. He pushed on the stick. The rotor blades above him whined louder. The landscape underneath him had no true shape at the extra five thousand feet he had climbed to. The cargo in the fuselage moaned louder. A slight smirk grew at the one corner of Charlie's mouth. He shook his head. His headset crackled. A burst of incoherent chatter ping ponged in his ears. He winced at the noise. Lifting a finger to quiet the noise in his own headset, he stopped from touching the volume control.

Can't risk not hearing the tower if I do that.

Instead he pushed his mike closer to his lips. "Everyone okay back there? We'll be landing in a few minutes. Need you to hold the chatter so I can hear the tower. You want me to land this bird safely, don't you?"

The helicopter went quiet. Only the whirl of the twin rotary blades whining echoed throughout. Charlie smiled. He glanced to his right.

A white gloved hand came into Charlie's peripheral view. It looked to be pointing out into the east coast. Charlie had gone to a few events over the years in the military where someone wore white gloves, but that mainly had to do with a ball—a Military ball. And today's events had no ball scheduled on it.

He huffed out a deep breath. His jaw grew tighter. For a brief moment he closed his eyes and shook his head.

You're an idiot for doing this.

He peeked over at his right side. The white gloved hand still pointed outward. "We're coming up to Dallas RBD. It won't be much longer."

The gloved hand pulled back.

If Susan ever found out his plans, she would skin him alive. Evie would probably disown him.

Lord allow me a day of success without problems. And if you could also allow it, would you please keep it all quiet? Thanks. Amen.

Out into the distance. Shapes took on more of
a business view.

Charlie turned in his seat. Juan Carlos sat to the right of him. The sun streaming into the chopper made the rainbow stripes glisten in his suit. The clown leaned back with one white gloved hand and arm draped on the door helping to hold his earphones in place. While looking directly at Charlie, he cocked his head toward the front window. With the flick of his finger he activated the microphone.

A burst of static shot through the earphones. Charlie winced behind his aviators. He breathed deep as the Spanish accented words came into his headset.

"Soon we will land at RBD, *sí?*"

Charlie nodded as he activated the microphone to his headset. "Yes. Almost there."

Juan Carlos smiled. "*Sí, gracias.*"

The radio chatter of Spanish grew louder in Charlie's headset. He groaned to himself. The chaos that battled in his head grew stronger. Spikes of pain stabbed every inch of his neck. Why he ever agreed to the idea of flying a group of clowns to the Dallas Executive heliport so they could make a connection with a jet to Bermuda at a private airfield had him questioning his own sanity. The antics going on behind him for the past thirty minutes couldn't be compared to his time in Mogadishu. Not that anything would ever compare to that period in his life, but this sure came close. No shells exploded around him. No bullets pierced the body of his Bell helicopter, but the noise, now that, he would compare to his days flying over Somalia. The screams of one of the clowns made him rethink ever having his doctor clean the wax out of his ears again. Then the moaning of another and gagging of one made his stomach twist. He rolled his eyes. He eased back on the stick.

A sharp crackle broke into the chatter that prompted him to look at the instrument panel in front of him. The clock indicated his need to signal air traffic control about his landing. At about twenty miles out it wouldn't be a problem, but anything less than fifteen then control did not appreciate it, especially if the flights in and out were heavy. But they would be landing at the RBD Executive heliport instead of DFW International airport, so with luck, it would be a quick drop off. A smirk appeared at the corner of Charlie's mouth.

Yeah, right. Lady luck didn't make the flight plan today, not especially with the chopper full of clowns.

Charlie blew out a breath and clicked on his microphone. "RBD Tower. This is Stockyard 1. Approaching RBD heliport, 3000 feet, about 15 miles southeast, request for landing."

"Roger, Stockyard 1, this is RBD Tower, about 15 miles out. Descent for your approach at 5 miles, three thousand feet."

"Stockyard 1, RBD Tower, five miles out, starting descent for approach to land."

Charlie pulled back on the stick as he adjusted the throttle. The chopper remained steady with his footwork applied to the yaw pedals.

"Okay, boys. We're about to land. Hold on to your hats."

When Charlie glanced over at Juan Carlos, the clown lifted his hand and gave him a white-gloved thumb up. Then peeking over his shoulder he chuckled to himself. The sight behind him might look horrific to most, but not Charlie. After all, white stony-faced passengers sometimes were a routine thing when it came to helicopters, especially military ones. He chuckled as the images of a few soldiers came into his memory with them turning a nice Missouri green bullfrog shade as his chopper would take off. Not many inexperienced soldiers flew in them, but once in a while he'd get one or two. Sometimes he might jostle the chopper a bit more just to have some fun and toughen up his crew, but not today. Well at least not on purpose. But by the looks of the clowns in the back with their partially made up faces like the rodeo clowns they used to be a few had a green tinge around the edge of their faces. Apparently the partial amount of clown make-up didn't come anywhere near covering up the discomfort. He wouldn't swear on it, but a few heads with hats, bandana, and a colorful wig or two had a gray cast to it.

He lifted his thumb to the group.

In all reality, Charlie had no particular problems with these guys, it's just that he hated clowns in general. And for them to unfortunately end up at the shelter, which he had an inkling that his dead brother-in-law had something to do with, it ended up being their own bad luck and not his. Heck, any troupe of clowns that landed on Evie's doorstep would get his undivided assistance in removing them from her life. And to know these clowns had some kind of connection with Josiah and the shelter and now possibly Miguel made Charlie's blood boil. He pulled back on the stick harder. The engines whined as the chopper lurched for the ground.

A collective gasp of terror reverberated off the walls of the fuselage.

Charlie jerked his shoulders as his eyes focused back on to the landscape.

Damn it. Get control of yourself.

He loosened his grip on the now sweaty stick. The color poured. back into his knuckles. The stick eased back to slow the descent.

Don't let them get to you. Less than fifteen minutes and they'll be out of our lives forever.

The helicopter floated down all while Charlie's weathered cowboy boots move gracefully like ballet slippers with enough pressure on the pedals so as to not make the chopper swing from side-to-side any more. With his free hand he adjusted the collective to throttle down the speed of the descent. Charlie's eyes narrowed to find the structure he aimed to land on. He licked his lips then with the flick of a finger he switched the microphone back on. "RBD Tower this is Stockyard 1, about five miles from RBD helipad, 1500 feet, request for descent to land."

"Stockyard 1, RBD Tower, Alpha platform one mile north west, approach with caution, three mile knot wind gusts."

"RBD Tower, one mile alpha platform northwest, wind gusts three mile nots, descent to land, approaching with caution."

"Stockyard 1, clear to land Alpha platform."

The dual deck elevated platform came into view. It lay in the central business center of Dallas just off the south end of the convention center.

Charlie maneuvered once around the helipad then centered the chopper just over its middle. He adjusted the throttle as he pulled back on the stick. His feet automatically moved in sync with his hands. He glanced at the instrument panel. All looked appropriate for the touchdown.

Almost down. Just a little bit further.

A shadow of darkness rolled over top. Thunder rolled overhead. A gust of wind followed in its wake. The bell lifted.

A collective gasp came from the back with one clown letting loose a muffled scream.

A thin film of perspiration appeared under Charlie's hairline. A smile cracked one side of his mouth upward

The shadow of dark clouds lingered above. Another gust blew over the landing pad.

Charlie shook his head. A low curse slid from his lips.

The crackle of his headset blanked out any remaining noise.

"*Cállnse.* Shh! *Señor* Charlie's got this."

A burst of pride exploded from Charlie's heart. Even though he'd had more difficult landings in his Military career, he still appreciated the confidence others had in him, even if it weren't the Military itself.

Charlie shot Juan Carlos a thumbs up then flicked on his mic. "Okay boys, ready to set her down. And remember no getting out until the blades stop."

No one spoke. But that didn't bother Charlie. In fact the quietness of the last few minutes he preferred. He chuckled to himself with the thought of maybe flying on days with chance of a storm would be best for transporting clowns, but shook his head at that thought.

This is a once in a lifetime flight. Nothing more.

The Bell hovered just above the landing spot. Charlie adjusted the throttle one last time and pulled back on the stick to lower the chopper. One runner touched. The helicopter leaned to its side. Charlie adjusted the tilt with his foot pedal dance. The Bell evened out with the other skid/runner touching down. He nodded to himself. "RBD Tower, this is Stockyard 1, touchdown on Alpha Platform confirmed."

"Stockyard 1, RBD Tower, Touchdown alpha platform confirmed, "nice job."

A loud cheer exploded from the back. Even the poodle barked its relief.

Charlie's earphones crackled. He glanced over to Juan Carlos.

Juan Carlos smiled. "They are very happy to be alive, *sí?*"

Charlie laughed. "*Sí, amigo,* they are."

Charlie flipped the switches to disengage the rotors. The blades slowed. No longer needing his headset for the moment, he pulled them off and tossed them onto the control panel. With the spent air in the cabin, he opened his door, which gave signal to the cargo their chance for escape. The back doors swung open. Cool air streamed into the fuselage.

When the rear silver and black chopper doors opened, a burst of cheers exploded from the chopper again. Five bodies tumbled out landing on the hot helipad. One by one, a colorful mismatched group of figures scrambled to stand. As they straightened their clothing and hats, the little black poodle came to the edge of the door and barked twice.

"Ay dios mío, Fifi."

The group separated to make room for the clown with a flowerpot-shaped hat. He turned and as soon as his arms went wide the poodle jumped. The clown's face lit up when he caught the dog and cuddled him into his arms. The dog snuggled under his chin.

A door slammed as another opened. The stern click of boots on the landing pad cut sharp over the final turns of the rotary blades.

The wind around the helicopter calmed.

But the commotion of the other clowns became frantic as the group pushed on each other to retrieve their bags.

The ding of an elevator rang out.

Charlie watched as the clowns froze. Not wanting to delay their departure any more than needed, he cupped a hand around his mouth. "Hurry. Their coming for you and your luggage."

In a synchronized pattern, the clowns turned toward him all at once with that same look of terror they had on their faces just before they landed. One might even say they probably thought he had taken them straight to the gallows.

Charlie rolled his eyes when he realized they thought they were done for. "No. It's the luggage cart. Load up and get going."

A remote-controlled luggage cart only a hair smaller than a manual cart pulled alongside the stunned clowns. The machine beeped then looked as if it powered down, but not before giving off two long beeps.

Charlie looked over at the elevator. The driver stood blocking the doors from sliding closed. Charlie gave him a thumbs up.

The controller nodded and tapped his wrist.

Charlie sighed as he turned back to the troupe of clowns and found them inspecting the cart. The little black poodle rolled around its floor while the flowerpot-hatted clown did a handstand on it.

The excitement of the remote controlled cart grew with the clowns. Two pulled out bubbles and began blowing them. Another blew on a party-horn blower. And the last one wearing a small cowboy hat waved a small red hanky in front of it like a matador.

Charlie froze. He shook his head.

Lord help me out here. Got to get them going otherwise they'll miss their flight.

The spikes poking into his neck resurfaced. He waved a hand. "Now boys, get your gear, you got to—"

Just then a loud crack broke the commotion.

As if they synchronized it, all heads turned toward the Bell.

Charlie's mouth hooked up to one side.

Thank you, Lord.

Juan Carlos stood near the tail of the chopper. One hand ungloved and pointed to the bags then the cart.

The clowns no longer moved or spoke. The crack snap of his fingers deactivated the little troupes' chaos. In fact, the only sound that one could hear in the background came from another chopper circling the helipad nearby.

Juan Carlos signaled to them without saying a word. And as his hand stopped moving, the energy of the troupe sprang alive. Each piled a bag onto the cart and then as a group they dashed toward the open elevator doors. The cart came alive with three beeps, jerked forward, then settled into a smooth roll and followed in the clowns wake.

Charlie tilted his head up but not before slipping his hand behind his neck to rub it. He closed his eyes briefly behind his aviators.

Lord thank you for getting us here safely and quickly. May this be the last time I ever see these clowns. Amen.

With no confirmation on Charlie's request, he leveled his view on Juan Carlos. He took a step forward, but not before he patted his chest to make sure the envelope he'd stuffed in his breast pocket hadn't fallen out. The sound of paper colliding with the inside of his leather jacket signaled everything could proceed as planned— as long as the clowns stuck to their part of the deal, then he would fulfill his.

The rainbow-suited clown sidled up next to Charlie.

A buzz from the elevator sounded in a hurried pattern.

Juan Carlos shook his head. "Sometimes I am loco for staying with them. *Sí?*"

Charlie chuckled. "The driver knows where to take you so you'll make your connection for Bermuda. Shouldn't take you more than a few hours to get you to your island."

Juan Carlos leaned toward Charlie with an outstretched hand. "Thank you for your help."

Charlie nodded, but before he shook the man's hand he reached into his pocket and pulled out the envelope. He slapped it between their palms. "I'd like to again thank you for helping me out with Evie."

Juan Carlos' hand curled around Charlie's and the envelope. "Anything, *mi amigo*."

Charlie nodded. A tightness to his throat settled making it difficult for any words. Mentally he shook off the last few hours if not days he had spent dealing with this troupe. But in all honesty, if he had to admit, he did like them. They seemed to be alright guys. They banded together like a troop of soldiers fighting or teasing one another, but working as a team when it counted. But, their lives depended on them clearing out. And his probably did too, especially if Susan found out. Not so much with Evie unless she discovered the check Juan Carlos gave her actually came from him. Then Susan might just hang him with his daughter's help.

Charlie smiled to himself.

Well, that just might get them talking again.

Juan Carlos gave Charlie's hand another squeeze. "Again, *gracias mi amigo*. We owe you our lives for getting us out of here sooner than planned."

Charlie released the envelope. "Let's just call it even." He tilted his head toward the envelope Juan Carlos now held. "But, that there is for all it's costing you to leave. It should be enough to help with a comfortable go at island life."

Juan Carlos stuffed the envelope into one of his pockets. "*Sí, Señor* Charlie."

"And you gave the other one to Evie?"

A large grin appeared on Juan Carlos' face. "*Sí*, after we talked at the coffee shop."

"Did you have any problems?"

Juan Carlos' brows scrunched together, then they slowly eased. "The coffee, she liked. The envelope, *no*."

Charlie pulled down on his glasses. "But she took it right?"

"*Sí*. She did."

The pinch of his nerves running up and down his neck started to ease.

"And remember no coming back. You hear?"

Juan Carlos nodded.

Charlie's eyes shot a look over at the elevator.

The wind kicked up as the distant sound of the circling chopper made its way closer.

All five of the clowns were waving and nodding.

He swiveled his eyes back to Juan Carlos' face. "And you tell that dead son of a gun brother-in-law of mine that if he ever steps foot back in Texas, I'll personally make sure he takes a real dirt nap. You got that?"

A smile poked at Juan Carlos mouth. "*Sí*. But I assure you, this is the last that Whiskey will hear of us."

Charlie's head dipped with his heart happy, but his brain pulled on his thoughts.

If Josiah's involved, I doubt it.

The buzz of the elevator broke the silence.

"They call for me. *Adiós, mi amigo*."

Charlie slapped the rainbow-suited clown on the shoulder. "*Adiós, mi amigo*."

And with that, Juan Carlos sprinted towards his troupe.

Charlie watched as The little rag-tag troupe of clowns disappear. With the doors closed and the light for the alpha pad dark now, he proceeded back to the Bell, but halted just before he rounded the chopper's nose.

Ding. Ding.

Charlie swiveled toward the bell. He cocked his head. The light for the Alpha pad's second elevator lit up. The heavy metal doors slid open.

The nerves in his neck tightened as the thought of the clowns returning crawled into his brain. Curse words slipped from his lips.

But instead, two dark haired men in black suits jogged toward him.

Charlie's eyebrows shot up.

The thinner man with a hard face with a stern jaw and blunt tone spoke behind a pair of mirrored sunglasses. "*Señor? Señor?* Wait. We need to speak."

Not sure who exactly they were talking to, Charlie scanned the platform as to make sure no one else stood there. Not finding anyone else, he turned and rested a hand on the nose of the Bell. He jabbed at his leather flight jacket. "Who, me?"

The older of the two and a much heavier man pushed on his glasses as he panted. "*Sí*."

Charlie studied the two as they came closer. He narrowed his gaze on them. A spark of something flickered in his memory, but at the moment he couldn't recall where he'd seen these two before. He blew out a breath and used the hand he rested on the chopper to prop himself up. "Howdy. What can I help you with?"

The thinner man halted just before Charlie while the heavier man stopped and bent for a few deep breaths.

Charlie watched as one scanned the other then the other.

The thinner man pointed to his chopper. "Did you just land?"

Charlie pulled his aviators down and peered over their edge. "And what business is it of yours?"

The thinner man threw his hands to his hips. "*Señor*, please, did you just land?"

Not sure exactly who these guys were or why they were here, he slowly turned to face them all while scratching his temple. "Land? Who wants to know and why?"

the thinner man blew out his breath and cursed in Spanish underneath his breath. His eyes narrowed in on Charlie. "Yes. You. Did you just land?"

Charlie's arm fell to his hip. "I did. And in fact lots of people land here." He pointed to one other chopper on the helipad. "One flew out before me and that one there had already landed." He pointed to the one circling the platform. "And that one there looks as if it wants to land before the storm."

The heavier set man frowned.

The thinner man rubbed a hand over his face and groaned.

Charlie started for the door of his Bell.

"*Señor?*"

Damn.

Charlie stopped, turned toward the men with a puckered face. "Yeah?"

"Did you bring clowns?"

With one eyebrow arched over his aviators, Charlie growled. "Clowns?"

The heavier man nodded. "*Sí*, clowns?"

Charlie jerked his head toward the back of the chopper. "Clowns? Seriously?" He pointed to his logo -- A longhorn head with the words The Stockyard arching over it glared back at them. "This here is a chopper for the Stockyard." He took a breath as the two men studied him. "If you don't know, that there ranch is one of the biggest in southeast Texas. Do you think we have time to haul clowns around in it?"

The thinner man leaned into his partner. A bit of Spanish floated between them. Too fast for Charlie to decipher, not that he knew much anyway, but he needed to go, but not before he gave the clowns an extra minute. So he did the next best thing. "We don't haul clowns in this Bell, but I'll tell you what, If you want, I can take you up and give you a good look of the landscape to see if you spot them anywhere. But we'll have to go quick, there's a storm brewing and I need to get back to my ranch. So what do you say? Want to take a whirl?"

Text Message
May 28th
7:00 PM

Charlie:	Darlin, want to meet Jack and Lila for drinks and dinner?
Charlie:	Darlin?
Susan:	Colonel Stockton, Mrs. Stockton is not taking yourmessages right now.
Charlie:	Who is then?
Susan:	Her assistant, Mary.
Charlie:	Tell you what Mary you tell her I'm not texting with any assistant of her's and if she doesn't take control of her phone, I'll meet Jack and Lila tonight without her or I could take you, but I'd prefer she come instead.
Susan:	Colonel Stockton at the moment right now I suggest you don't kid. She's got a very deadly look in her eye.
Charlie:	Is it one that looks like sparks are flying?
Susan:	Yes.
Charlie:	I love that look. Now get her on here or I'll come there and we'll really make the sparks fly.
Charlie:	Mary?
Charlie:	Susan?
Susan:	Charles Joseph Stockton, don't you dare come here. I'm so mad I could skewer you with a pitchfork.
Charlie:	Hello Darlin, anyone ever tell you that you're sexy when you text mad?
Susan:	Yes. And this is not funny.
Charlie:	Wait, what? Who?
Susan:	The @$$ of a Colonel I married.
Charlie:	Well, that's fine. If it's only him. Thought I might have to take someone out behind the woodshed tonight.
Susan:	Get serious. We don't have a woodshed.
Charlie:	Okay, how about the barn then?
Susan:	Charles!
Charlie:	Come on Darlin' ease up on that anger.

Susan: I'm rather ticked with you. Rumor at the office says Evie won
            that eminent domain case

Charlie: Well, I'll be a monkey's uncle.

Susan: Charles! This is not funny.

Charlie: Hey, now. That's no way to look at it.

Susan: And how should I?

Charlie: Still working on that.

Susan: Oh, that figures.

Charlie: Give me a minute…

Susan: Times up. Now why shouldn't I be mad?

Charlie: Why not make the shelter one of the Foundation's charity?

Charlie: Susan?

Susan: Possibly. But, I'm still mad at you!

Charlie: Maybe. But you can't stay mad forever.

Susan: Want to try me?

Charlie: Darlin'?

Susan: Just how long is forever?

Charlie: Our time now and eternity in heaven.

Charlie: Susan?

Susan: I'm thinking.

Charlie: What if I bribe you with a new pair of those fancy boots?

Susan: You already did that. Think of something else.

Charlie: You sure a night out with Jack and Lila won't do it?

Susan: Are you drinking now?

Charlie: How about going to Loveland with me?

Susan: Colorado?

Charlie: That's the place.

Susan: Does this count as our getaway trip?

Charlie: Do you want it to?

Susan: Does this mean you need a new horse? Or a saddle?

Charlie: Horse.

Susan: You need a new horse?

Charlie: No, Jack does.

Susan: What? Jack? Seriously?

Charlie: Galloped on to the great pasture in the sky.

Susan: Foreshadowing.
Charlie: Not in the least. That old buzzard will be around for a long time.
Susan: Not if Lila has anything to say about that.
Charlie: Doesn't Evie know a vet up there?
Susan: The one from Texas A&M?
Charlie: That's the one.
Susan: Why?
Charlie: Call Evie and get the number for me.
Susan: Seriously?
Charlie: Come on Darlin', don't be stubborn.
Susan: I'm still not happy with you.
Charlie: I know. We'll talk when you get home.
Susan: Why? You won't help me.
Charlie: You two will have to talk someday.
Susan: Never mind. I'll be late.
Charlie: No worries. I'll wait… always.
Susan: Always?
Charlie: Yes, always!
Susan: Sweet talker.
Charlie: Only for my bride.

Chapter 18 Whiskey Coffee

CHARLIE FIGURED HE'D HAVE TO have it out once and for all sooner or later with Susan. And it looked as if it were going to be sooner than later. So he figured the best place to have this conversation would be in his office—on his turf. He knew if he had the upper hand when it came to Susan, he had a better chance of her understanding his view on the whole matter. Plus, while he waited, he could have a cup of coffee.

After all, he never went on a mission without having a cup of coffee for some fortitude. Well, maybe not fortitude, but definitely caffeine to keep his mind sparking on all cylinders. In all honesty, he wanted this whole matter with Evie and Susan to be done with. And for that, he needed to get rid of the clowns and help with an infusion of cash to get the shelter up on its feet again. And since Charlie had been able to do just that, Susan had no reason to keep Evie from doing what she had her heart set on. At least, that's what he told himself.

Not one who could sit behind his desk for long periods of time, Charlie grabbed his coffee mug and walked over to the picture window that looked out on The Stockyard. The pasture in front of him rolled for miles. The longhorns that rambled across the field worked at a steady pace with the help of his cowhands. He blew out his breath. He wanted to be out there, but at the moment he couldn't. Not that he couldn't, but he needed to resolve this whole issue between Susan and Evie first and foremost.

The muscles in his neck tightened.

He leaned against the frame of the picture window and closed his eyes. He lifted his chin.

Lord. Need your help here. Still not sure how to handle this whole situation, so if you could send me a signal. I'd right kindly appreciate it. Amen.

As the Texas sun shone through the window, the heat of the rays warmed his skin even with the day growing late. He breathed in deep.

Charlie cringed.

The strong aroma of spice and fruit rose from the cup of coffee he held. He hadn't paid too much attention to it until the scent prickled his nose just now.

With a cocked eyebrow, Charlie tilted the cup for a better peek at the hot liquid. He hadn't noticed until a moment ago that this coffee held a rather peculiar smell, which smelled nothing like his usual robust brew. This smelled more like a stale fruitcake. In fact, as he examined the liquid, he realized the mug he held didn't resemble anything like his traditional brown mug either. No, in fact it looked totally different.

Charlie tipped back his hat. The mug he held closer displayed a colorful assortment of figures. One corner of Charlie's lips curled up. He laughed to himself as he twisted the cup around. He took another sniff of the coffee. The cinnamon and orange-spiced coffee took on a whole new meaning for him. Plus this particular scent reminded him of a time when he flew alongside Mexico. His co-pilot at the time loved coffee too, especially coffee from a little cantina over the border. They made a spicy fruit flavored coffee that his co-pilot had to have every day. But not Charlie, he loved a good old hardy straight-up black coffee. He needed nothing fancy for his cup of java.

He twisted the cup once more. The figures on the mug resembled a collection of around the world clowns. And in a strategic spot a Mexican clown smiled right at the holder of the mug.

Right then and there, Charlie's heart gave a little kick. He would have to check with Lucia to see where the coffee came from and the mugs, but his heart told him the gesture came from his passengers who he flew his last trip over to the Dallas Executive Heliport. He figured the gesture in not so many words meant a grateful thanks for getting them out of Texas.

Charlie nodded at the clown on the cup. "You're welcome." Then with a long drink of the cinnamon spiced orange flavored coffee he leaned against the frame of the window. The coffee slid down his throat as he closed his eyes.

A slight curve of his lips curled up. The idea that the clowns were no longer a problem eased some of the tension in his neck.

Yes, he managed to get them out of town safely, and in fact on to their own tropical island. No one needed to worry about them anymore. Miguel would finish his sentence then join the others. And the others, well, they were officially retired now. The little circus had disbanded and the troupe of clowns had flew off toward the sunset. Well, more like Bermuda, not the sunset.

Regardless of the facts, they were now gone. And unless, a certain "dead" brother-in-law showed up out of the blue, he figured the clowns would stay put.

Charlie did chew on the inside of his cheek for a moment when the image of the two Mexicans from the heliport meandered straight into the middle of his thoughts. Unable to figure them out, he hoped they'd given up on the Clowns. Plus, he'd managed to help Evie out financially with the clowns' assistance so all seemed good there. And he liked the fact that his best friend's nephew, Griff had taken a strong interest in his daughter. One that looked promising, if the boy didn't screw it up… again.

Charlie shook his head.

Lord, help that boy. He's a smart one, but he does come from that Barleyshot stock of Jack's. Amen.

With the tension easing up and his mug just under his nose, he closed his eyes and inhaled. The robust notes of the spice and fruit scents were quite strong, the idea of saving the rest until morning, which would definitely be an eye opener rode into his thoughts. But with the last bit he needed to do to finish up this matter with Evie and Susan, he figured he'd need to finish tonight with a strong cup of coffee. And with the arrival of the new blend, he figured with its energetic aroma it would do the trick.

Not that he considered what he had in mind physically tough like in the Army, but mentally, it probably rivaled it if not more. After all, there weren't many times when in the Army did he go without coffee or head-to-head with a worthy opponent like his wife, because he had to remember she had made Mae Foundation into a top Fortune one-hundred company and no one got their on their looks.

Charlie smiled to himself

Yes sir, she's quite the beauty, but she'd kick anyone's a$$ if they thought that's how she got where she's at today.

So when it came to what he needed to get done like any mission he manned before, he made it a staple to have packed in their gear when they flew out on any mission. He considered it an essential part that fueled his nerves to get the job done.

And for what he had to do tonight, not that it had anything to do with the Military, it would require that same bit of fortitude for his nerves to get the matter handled. Not that he would drink a whole pot right now, but maybe another cup. After all, he didn't have the time for a whole pot, but another cup, yes, now that he could manage.

And for what would probably take place as soon as Susan arrived, he'd need some of that fortitude. Because his wife knew how to get to him. And he'd do anything for her. Normally that would be okay, but this whole thing with Evie just didn't sit well with him. So ,he needed something potent, something to build up his fortitude. And the stronger the better. In fact, he wouldn't be opposed to any coffee that took the hair off one's chest.

Charlie took a large gulp.

Almost immediately, his throat tightened. He coughed as if he needed to clear his throat. The heat and strength of the brew burned a pathway down his throat that moved as slow as tar.

Wetness hung onto his eyes. A light sweat formed underneath his cowboy hat.

He examined the cup as he swirled the contents. Not sure what he expected to see rise up out of the bottom, but if the remnants of a pitchfork appeared, it would not surprise him.

The briefest thought of the clowns trying to pay him back with such a spicy blend for the flight over to the heliport crossed his mind.

Charlie rolled his eyes and reminded himself that the ridiculous clowns were no longer any threat. And now, the only real problem he had to fix would be the differences that spurred up between mother and daughter.

Voices sounded in the hall.

Charlie glanced over his shoulder. No one appeared in the door.

He turned back to the picture window and watched the cowhands work the longhorns. He studied the interaction of the cowhands and the herd.

For the most part, the longhorns meandered over the field heading toward the barn. But within a split second, one cowboy took off with lasso in the air and landing it around a rambunctious calf's neck that broke free from the herd.

The cowboy slowly pulled on the lasso enough to haul the youngster back over near its mama where she stood grazing on some tall blades of grass.

"Nice job."

Then he spotted two cowhands gently guiding a young heifer back to the heard. No rope, no prod, just their horses to steer her back.

Charlie took a sip of his coffee.

The young heifer slid back into the ranks of the herd. The cowhands followed on the outskirts. They rode only far enough away so not to bother the flow, but yet close enough to lend a hand when needed.

And at that moment, the solution to his problem hit him.

With a glance upward, His lips curled.

Okay, Lord. I get it now.

Not until what he just witnessed, had Charlie known for sure what he needed to do. But thanks to the Lord's subtlety, the answer hit him in the form of his cowhands and his longhorns. Why he hadn't realized it before, but at the moment, he wanted to kick himself for not knowing the basics of raising a family.

In all reality, when it came to Susan and their daughter, and the trouble that stirred between the two, he would have liked to avoid this part, but knowing it had finally caught up to him and tossed him in the middle, he figured better now to deal with it. Putting it off wouldn't make it fade away. And the fairness to his wife could no longer be avoided. In fact it would probably make things worse if he ignored it. In spite of everything, hadn't he done that for the past thirty years? Well, sort of, instead of ignoring it, he left Susan to deal with it. But now the time had come to step up and straighten out this mess once and for all.

The tap of high heels came down the hall.

Charlie leaned one shoulder against the picture window.

The cadence of those heels would be none other than his wife.

He cocked his head and listened with more intensity.

Her step came smooth and succinct.

The footsteps finally halted at the door.

Energy snapped in the room.

No one spoke.

Charlie made no turn toward the door. His gaze remained on the pasture. He waited to make his move. After all, he believed the best offense took on a good defense.

With the lift of the mug, he took another drink.

The tapping heels approached.

"Charles?"

Even though he recognized the voice, Charlie remained quiet.

More energy crackled.

Prickles stirred on his neck nerves.

Not many would guess that an argument hovered between the two, but Charlie had done things his way with regards to Evie and the clowns this time and had completely ignored all of Susan's requests.

Positive his wife had figured out what he'd done, he'd need to brace for the fight.

After all, she would be mad. No not mad, furious would be more like it.

She wanted the whole matter handled her way, not Charlie's. And of course why wouldn't she? He knew she ran the household and their businesses for the past thirty years while he served in the Army. So relinquishing any kind of control wouldn't be any option she'd take.

And, Susan would see this as a big disappointment in him and in all honesty, he could live with that. But what he couldn't live with would be having Evie under thumb all her life. She'd had enough of that. The strings needed cut, but it didn't mean he'd let his daughter stray too far without helping if she needed it.

Time to do it. Let's get this over with. Better for everyone.

In spite of everything, Charlie understood disappointment. It isn't as if he'd truly chosen this path he now traveled on. In fact, he'd always hoped to retire one day as a five star general, but that never came to fruition. Although if one looked at him now, they'd see he owned one of the largest cattle ranches in East Texas, if not the whole state. He chuckled to himself.

And I'm still alive, only gored once, so maybe cattle rustling isn't so bad.

He took the last gulp of his coffee and waited.

The tap of high heels came closer. The light touch of a hand curled around his biceps. Charlie's heart kicked. He sucked in his breath. The air in the room tossed around the notes of a robust Mexican coffee and the delicate scent of a perfume. Both intoxicated him, but in all honesty, the light fragrance won out.

With the coffee mug emptied, Charlie pushed a few silver picture frames back on the windowsill and eased the mug on to the sill. With the tilt of his head and the turn of his body, Charlie faced the love of his life.

"Charles?"

For a half second, he studied his wife. The dark power suit and matching heels exuded strength, but when her eyes twinkled like they did now with a grey blue pattern that accentuated the few streaks of silver that highlighted her fading auburn tresses only reminded him of what they've had together all these years. The pride that swelled into his whole body couldn't be explained at the moment, if ever. He figured no one else would understand unless they'd walked in his shoes.

The corner of Charlie's mouth hitched up. His heart kicked again. The longing to place a kiss on her lips grew from his heart. And this time, his heart wanted no little peck on the cheek, it wanted the real thing. He leaned into her and tilted her chin up so that their lips lay only a whisper away.

"Yes, Darlin'."

The hint of a smirk peaked out from behind Charlie's fingers. "What were you thinking?"

"Thinking? Isn't it obvious?"

He stared into her eyes. "Would I surprise you if I said you?"

Susan pulled back, a slight wash of pink colored her cheeks, but not enough to make her turn and run. Instead, she stood toe-to-toe with him with hands firmly planted on her hips. "Charles. I'm serious."

Confusion crept into Charlie's thoughts. Not sure what his wife referred to now, but he assumed he'd made it obvious with the touch to her chin and the intimate whispers, but apparently not. Somehow, his signals now resembled tangled barbwire.

"Charles. I understand why you got those clowns away from Evie."

Charlie's brow lifted. His gut tightened.

Lord, please don't let her know the truth. I don't think I could handle that wrath right now.

"Clowns? You know about the clowns at the shelter? The ones at Evie's shelter?"

Susan cringed. "I do. I also appreciate you convincing them to move on. But, maybe if they'd stayed a little longer, Evie would have realized she's not cut out for that sort of life."

"Hmm?" Charlie rubbed the back of his neck. No icepick tingles. No hair standing.

Susan folded her arms over her chest. "Don't you see? At the Foundation we can shield her from things like this. That shelter will cause her to have a nervous breakdown."

Charlie calmly told himself to have patience. Susan's reaction came as a protective mamma. Not one of controlling. After all, she lived through the kidnapping of her only daughter some twenty years ago. And Charlie's absence hadn't helped when each time he went back on duty. His heart ached thinking of all those years. But in all reality, when it came to Evie's safety, they could relax now. He'd made sure of it. He understood her protectiveness. But he knew she had to be set free. Someone caged could never flourish. And that he wouldn't stand for, not for his daughter.

Hold your ground, man.

Charlie blew out his breath. He slowly shook his head. "Susan, Darlin', just let it go."

"But—"

Charlie held up a hand. A nerve in his jaw twitched. "Now stop. She's safe. Griff will make sure. And the clowns won't return."

The energy between them snapped and crackled.

Susan's arms fell to her side as she stomped her foot. "But you don't know that."

Charlie groaned. Caught between the truth and a lie that had ensnared him thanks to his not so dead brother-in-law, Charlie had to make a decision. Tell Susan the truth or let the lie bury the truth. Which would be worse? Allow Susan to think her only brother had died in a plane over the Bermuda Triangle? Or ruin a number of people's lives?

Charlie blew out his breath.

Lord, please forgive me, but I believe what I'm about to do is the best for everyone.

Charlie narrowed his eyes on Susan. "Stop. Don't stir up trouble where there is none."

"But— but—"

Charlie growled. "The clowns left. In fact, they retired. Griff's with her. And that boy isn't about to let her out of his sight."

A frown tugged at Susan's lips. "But what about the future?"

Charlie rolled his eyes. "As for the Foundation, it's your dream. Not hers. Let her be. We haven't lost her forever, but if you keep pushing it I just might join her."

Susan's eyes went wide. "Charles, you wouldn't?"

A little kick to Charlie's heart caught some notice.

Hmm?

What exactly that meant, he couldn't be sure. But he had no problem exploring it.

The sparks in the air took on a new kind of crackle.

Under normal circumstances, he knew he'd never get away with what he wanted to do now, but when the time called for drastic measures to divert Susan's attention away from Evie, the clowns, and her brother, he decided this would not be the best time to waste such an opportunity. And when his heart spoke, rarely did he have the chance to do anything but to surrender to its wishes. And at the moment, Charlie's heart took charge of this battle.

So with one fluid movement, he reached around Susan, caught her by the waist, and yanked her into his chest. His head lowered so that his jaw rubbed against her ear. "Grrr. You aren't getting rid of me that easy."

"Charles, my makeup."

"Oh for heaven's sake, Susie, forget the makeup once." Then he dipped her backwards.

The look of shock softened on Susan's face. The hint of a giggle caught in her throat. She tried to shake it off. "Charlie—"

But not willing to give in, he nuzzled her neck. "Darlin', forget about the makeup for one minute."

Susan made no reply. In fact, she lay in his arms without movement.

Charlie chuckled to himself knowing his wife lay just on the edge of losing control. He knew when she got quiet, she battled with her self-control.

Charlie pulled back and studied her.

Her eyes closed, but he knew, her telltale sign came when she bit just a tiny part of her bottom lip. Not many people would notice it, but Charlie always did. And sure enough, he spotted only a hint of ivory teeth biting into her lip.

Charlie's heart kicked again. He knew with a little encouragement the right way would change her mind. She might not go willing on everything, but she'd eventually agree with him. Charlie's love for his wife wrapped tighter around his heart. A sure tell sign that only Susan held his heart. And it had always been her to do this even if her stubbornness got in the way. But he knew how to work her stubbornness to his advantage. So to get what he wanted he leaned closer. Only a whisper breath away he growled. "Darlin', come on, Sugar, don't make me beg."

A little giggle slipped past Susan's lips as one eye peaked open, then the other. Finally, she whispered. "Okay but just for now."

Charlie's brows furrowed. "For now?"

Another giggle slipped out. "Okay, for you."

"And what about Evie?"

Almost immediately Susan's grip on Charlie's shirt tightened. No more giggles escaped her lips. Her eyes slammed shut.

Charlie watched as she closed up on him. But not willing to let her go, he nuzzled his nose against hers. His words came out low and playful. "Darlin, do it for me, please."

Susan didn't push away. She didn't struggle to get free. Instead she licked her bottom lip and pulled him as close as to a whisper could ever get. "Only because I love you, Charlie."

And on those words, his brain branded Susan's name to his heart. Not wanting to waste the moment, Charlie moved in for a deep kiss.

The air between them sizzled.

The pulse in his neck pounded like a wild horse. He tightened his grip around her waist. His prickled neck muscles disappeared. Relief swept through him as her body melted against his. The distance between their lips disappeared. "You'll always have my heart. And for that I love you, Darlin'."

Text Message

May 31st
1:04 PM

Charlie:	Everything okay?
Evie:	Yes. All good. Except…
Charlie:	Except what?
Evie:	Do we have any old Polaroids of Uncle Josiah?
Charlie:	Josiah? Polaroids? Why?
Evie:	Now found a second polaroid of Uncle Josiah.
Charlie:	Second one?
Evie:	Yep, someone's leaving polaroids of him at the shelter.
Charlie:	Anything else with them?
Evie:	No, not with this one. But the first one came with fudge.
Charlie:	When'd you get the first one?
Evie:	After the clowns came.
Charlie:	You sure?
Evie:	Yes. What are you thinking?
Charlie:	I'm thinking you need to send me a copy.
Evie:	Will you show them to Mother?
Charlie:	No. Don't need her getting upset.
Evie:	I agree. On another note, ever fly to Bermuda?
Charlie:	No. Too far by chopper.
Evie:	And there's that triangle, too. Right?
Charlie:	Right. Signing off. Coffee is getting cold.

THE END

Howdy Friend,

I wanted to take a moment to thank you from the bottom of my heart for taking the time to read this contemporary western romance novella, Cherishing Whiskey's Salvation from my Whiskey Salvation series.

As a blind author, writing is my way of painting pictures with words, and your thoughts mean the world to me. If you enjoyed the ride, I'd be mighty grateful if you could leave a review on Goodreads, Amazon, or where ever you purchased your copy. Even better yet, asking your local libraries to carry my books would be a dream come true. And if not, I'd still like to hear from you so I know how to improve. Feel free to contact me through e-mail at

chrissyhartmann@sssnet.com

Thanks again for being the best reader a cowboy-loving writer could ask for. Your support truly makes a difference.

Happy trails,

Chrissy Hartmann

Review Links:

Amazon

https://amazon.com/review/create-review?asin=B0BTBLC6T5

Good Reads

https://www.goodreads.com/book/show/122897327-cherishing-whiskey-s-salvation

ABOUT THE AUTHOR

Chrissy lives with the two loves of her life, her hubby and son in a sleepy college town in Northeast Ohio. Growing up in farm country tipping cows, riding horses, and surviving the depths of Lake Erie on a 36-foot sailboat have given her plenty of experiences to fill her books with a whole slew of unique characters. Their all from her imagination, an imagination some say like Dr. Frankenstein where she throws together bits and pieces of the people she's met into one creation.

She loves to write and can usually be found doing just that about any time of the day, except when her hubby does manage to pull her away to go for a ride to get ice cream or spin vinyl in the basement. Even though she's always working on her writing or studying history, she makes plenty of time for Star Wars with her Eagle Scout son. Heck, she's even been caught discussing her favorite Corellia smuggler all while they wrestle down their disgruntled long-haired kitten, Punkin to get out the knots she manages to snare.

Chrissy loves to venture out with her dog guide, Winnie especially to her writers group and writing conferences. Her favorite local spots are to the library and a coffee shop to get her daily dose of caffeine, especially when it's pumpkin season, then its pumpkin everything. So buy her a refill and have a chat. Who knows, parts of your life might end up in one of her contemporary romances or even as a quirky character in a short story.

You can find Chrissy at https://chrissyhartmann.com

A list of her books can be found at https://chrissyhartmann.com/books

And you can find more of Chrissy's book merchandise on her website at https://ChrissyHartmann.com/Extras/

To read the latest news, sign up for her newsletter at https://prickleforrestchronicles.com/follow-me

Don't forget to follow her on Instagram, Facebook, and Twitter by following her at USAWriter355.

Coming Soon…

Book three to the Whiskey Salvation Series. And remember her Whiskey Salvation Cookbook,

Cowboy Up With Grapeseed Oil; Heartfelt Recipes With Benefits

…Follow and subscribe to find out more https://chrissyhartmann.com/blog

Thanks and enjoy!